FOR ALL WE KNOW

● ● ●

ONE STRIKE AWAY BOOK THREE

● ● ●

MARY J. WILLIAMS

ABOUT THE AUTHOR

Writing isn't easy. But I love every second. A blank screen isn't the enemy. It is the opportunity to create new friends and take them on amazing adventures and life-changing journeys. I feel blessed to spend my days weaving tales that are unique—because I made them.

Billionaires. Songwriters. Artists. Actors. Directors. Stuntmen. Football players. They fill the pages and become dear friends I hope you will want to revisit again and again.

Thank you for jumping into my books and coming along for the journey.

<u>HOW TO GET IN TOUCH</u>

Please visit me at these sites, sign up for my newsletter or leave a message.

http://www.maryjwilliams.net/

https://www.facebook.com/maryjwilliamsauthor/?ref=hl

https://twitter.com/maryjwilliams05

https://www.pinterest.com/maryj0675/

https://www.instagram.com/2015romance/

https://www.goodreads.com/author/show/5648619.Mary_J_Willia ms

MORE BOOKS BY MARY J. WILLIAMS

Harper Falls Series

If I Loved You

If Tomorrow Never Comes

If You Only Knew

If I Had You (Christmas in Harper Falls)

Hollywood Legends Series

Dreaming With a Broken Heart

Dreaming With My Eyes Wide Open

Dreaming Again

Dreaming of a White Christmas

(Caleb and Callie's story)

One Pass Away Series

After the Rain

After All These Years

After the Fire

Hart of Rock and Roll

Flowers on the Wall

Flowers and Cages

Flowers are Red

Flowers for Zoe

One Strike Away

For a Little While

For Another Day

WITH ONE MORE LOOK AT YOU

TABLE OF CONTENTS

PROLOGUE 1

CHAPTER ONE 10

CHAPTER TWO.. 25

CHAPTER THREE 36

CHAPTER FOUR.. 44

CHAPTER FIVE... 58

CHAPTER SIX... 70

CHAPTER SEVEN 84

CHAPTER EIGHT 99

CHAPTER NINE... 108

CHAPTER TEN 125

CHAPTER ELEVEN 133

CHAPTER TWELVE.. 142

CHAPTER THIRTEEN 153

CHAPTER FOURTEEN 166

CHAPTER FOURTEEN 179

CHAPTER FIFTEEN.. 202

CHAPTER FIFTEEN 220

CHAPTER SIXTEEN 241

CHAPTER SEVENTEEN 252

EPILOGUE 265

PROLOGUE

● ≈ ● ≈ ●

THE LAST TIME Travis Forsythe felt the power of a motorcycle between his legs was the last time he set foot in Green Hills, South Carolina.

Eleven years by everyday standards. By Travis' way of thinking, more like a lifetime. He left Green Hills a kid without a dime to his name. Even the beat-up old Kawasaki he'd tenderly nursed along through high school, decided thirty miles down the road to finally give up the ghost, dying with little ceremony.

Travis hadn't blinked. Though he cursed up a blue streak, he sure as hell didn't turn back. Blessed with a strong body and a will of iron, he walked, the worn heels of his just-this-side-of-too-tight leather boots crunching in the loose gravel. The old duffle bag taxed with carrying his earthly possessions slung over one shoulder.

Luckily, Travis didn't own much, making his burden light. And with each step, the weight—from the bag, from his soul—lifted more and more. He swore then and there that if he failed—fell unceremoniously on his face—he'd never come back.

A promise he'd kept. Until now.

1

As Travis parked the Harley—black, shiny, and brand new off the showroom floor—on the street, any changes to Green Hills were lost on him. He didn't care enough to notice.

He recalled the words he'd said to Nick Landers the day before as they parted company in New York.

In and out. Travis had one piece of business on his agenda. Then he'd be off to Bermuda. After a long, sometimes grueling, yet ultimately triumphant baseball season, he and Nick deserved a little R&R.

Good company. Cold drinks. Hot beaches. Hotter women. Blonde, brunette, or redhead? If the mood struck—and the ladies were willing—perhaps all three at the same time.

Grinning at the idea, Travis removed his helmet, running a hand through his thick, dark hair that—much to his chagrin as a boy—tended to curl at the ends. What he needed was a haircut.

Travis would find a barber shop in Bermuda. One looking out over the ocean, not an alleyway like the one his father used to take him to in Green Hills. He wanted a place where the air was clean, not clogged with the smell of rotten garbage, piss, and God knows what else.

Five minutes in this town and his mind had already headed south, dredging up memories he hadn't thought about in years.

Gripping the helmet with leather-clad hands, Travis shook off his wayward musings. He paused outside the storefront to take a deep, centering breath. Like stepping up to the plate, bottom of the ninth, a runner on second, his team down a run. Focus. Eliminate all distractions.

See the ball.

Or in this case, focus on fixing an annoying problem.

Travis gave the building a cursory inspection. As always, his blue gaze missed little. Though the faded white paint peeled from around the window frame, the plate glass sparkled—not a speck of dirt or a smudge to be seen. And the sign above the door—the big, bold lettering a cheery red—looked brand spanking new.

Green Hills Non-Profit Thrift Shop. All donations welcome.

Travis had a donation. A swift kick to the proprietor's backside.

Three heads turned as Travis entered the building. The pretty brunette checking out a display of dishes sent him a warm, *who do we have here*, smile. Not as friendly, the older man and woman sorting through a rack of winter coats eyed him with a faint air of suspicion.

Seemed about right for a small town, Travis thought. *Any* small town. Green Hills didn't have the monopoly on flirty *or* suspicious.

The fourth person in the room, just out of her teens—maybe— didn't have time to worry about Travis. She stood behind the counter—near an old-fashioned cash register—working the life out of a piece of gum, the contents of a dog-eared book holding her complete attention.

The woman Travis wanted to see was nowhere to be found. Naturally. Why make his visit any easier?

Logically, Travis knew—since he hadn't sent word to expect him—his anger wasn't warranted. So what? Since when did logic and anger go hand in hand?

He was here. Where the hell was she?

Rather than stew, Travis did what he always did. He took action.

"Excuse me?"

"All the items are clearly marked." Without raising her eyes, the young woman flicked a lock of purple-streaked hair over her shoulder. "The next best price is free. And we don't do free."

Travis admired a woman with attitude. Downright rude was something else. She needed a lesson in customer relations. But he had neither the time—nor inclination.

"I don't care about your prices. I'm looking for—"

"Hello, Travis."

Delaney Pope.

Though much about her had changed in eleven years, Travis would have known her anywhere the second he looked into her eyes. Those big, amazing, startlingly bright, purple eyes.

"We need to talk." Noting the sudden interest from the gum-chomping cashier, Travis added, "Alone."

"My office is in the back."

As he followed Delaney, Travis noted the sway of her hips—hips he was certain she hadn't possessed the last time they met. A twinge of unease made his gaze shift until he reminded himself about the passage of time. She wasn't a kid any longer.

No, he decided, Delaney was a woman. In every sense of the word.

Like Travis, she hadn't lived their time apart in a bubble. She had grown up. He could admire her figure without feeling guilt. And, without the slightest intention of acting on the automatic attraction.

Sorry, brain. Sometimes his libido ran the show. The age-old man/woman thing—no matter the woman or their history—couldn't be tamped down.

Delaney took a seat behind an old wooden desk, pockmarked with long, deep scars. A shaft of sunlight from the small back window landed on a small wastebasket, filled with wadded-up pieces of paper.

Her gaze, when she finally met his, was steady. A little cool, but hardly glacial. As if they had parted that morning instead of eleven years ago.

"What can I do for you?"

"You want to play dumb?"

"I couldn't if I tried. Remember?" Delaney tapped her temple with a scarlet-colored nail. "Genius."

Irritated, Travis crossed his arms. When they were teenagers, one glance at his intractable stance and Delaney would have crumbled. Now, she didn't blink. She wasn't intimidated. Or afraid. Here stood a woman who could hold her own. The woman he'd always known she could be.

"Brains doesn't always equal common sense, Del."

"I'm not foolish, Travis." Delaney raised a brow, almost daring him to contradict her. "Nor can you come in here and throw your weight around. You once helped me find the strength to fight back. Now, I don't need anybody's help."

"I gave you a nudge back then. The rest was all you."

A flicker of emotion—the first she'd shown—warmed her gaze. "You gave me more than a nudge, Travis. You gave me something—someone—to hold onto when I thought I was about to drown."

Words weren't necessary. Neither had forgotten. Which led Travis back to why he was there.

"Do you want to explain this?"

Travis placed a cashier's check on the desk.

"I owed you money." Delaney shrugged. "Now I don't."

"Stubborn," Travis mumbled.

"All depends on your point of view. You say stubborn. I say pragmatic. We had unfinished business. That check wipes the slate clean."

Taking a deep breath, Travis rubbed his temples, counting slowly to ten. He really, really needed a vacation.

"All the time we knew each other. Through everything, I only asked two things."

"Travis—"

"Never pay me back," Travis interrupted. "And never, never, return to Green Hills."

"That day is burned in my memory, Travis. But, you can't hold me to promises made when I was fifteen and scared out of my mind. Scared for both of us."

Without effort, Travis could see Delaney—the picture he'd held dear for so long—as she'd looked in her blue dress, a length of white satin ribbon holding back her hair. Her eyes the color of soft, purple velvet.

Delaney wasn't the only one whose memory was burned that day.

"Nothing's changed, Del."

"You're wrong." Delaney's hands clenched. As if realizing, she breathed deeply, relaxing her fingers. "Everything has changed. Me, especially. I don't need your money. And I don't need you to take care of me. Not anymore."

"Funny," Travis said. "The way I remember things, we took care of each other. We were friends."

"*Were* is the operative word, Travis. Those days are long gone."

"I still think of you as a friend."

Travis felt a tug of regret when he saw surprise flare in Delaney's eyes. He could have—*should* have—stayed in touch. He hadn't forgotten her as much as pushed her to the back of his mind. So much happened so quickly. He hadn't been able to process the mess. Truthfully, he still hadn't. Not completely.

He had a good life. Damn near perfect. More money and success than he'd dreamed possible. Which said something. From an early age, Travis' dreams had always leaned toward the colossal.

From the looks of her, Delaney seemed to have her shit together. If the check she'd sent him was any indication, money wasn't a problem. She'd bloomed into a gorgeous, confident, young woman.

Why tempt fate by dredging up the past?

"Friends who haven't spoken in over a decade?" Delaney scoffed. "I don't think so. You have no right to try to dictate what I do with my money or where I choose to spend my time."

"No right?"

"None whatsoever."

Travis rested his hands on the desk, leaning forward. Close enough to see the flecks of silver that highlighted the unusual color of her eyes.

"My rights as a delinquent friend may be debatable. But there's one thing you can't deny."

Delaney crossed her arms over her chest, the look she gave him said her patience had almost run its course.

"Do tell. What rights could you possibly have over me?"

Travis slowly smiled, knowing he held the winning card.

"My rights as your husband."

CHAPTER ONE

● ≈ ● ≈ ●

ELEVEN YEARS EARLIER

● ● ●

"YOU'LL SURVIVE ANOTHER four months."

"But a chance like this might not come along again."

"Six months, Travis. Get your high school diploma. That's all I ask. After graduation, you can do whatever you want."

The frustration that lately seemed at a constant low boil, ticked up a few degrees. Travis knew what his father wanted—no matter what he said.

"You want me to pick college over playing ball."

Alan Forsythe picked up an old, dented toolbox. The same one he'd used for as long as Travis could remember. Every day, like clockwork, Alan headed out the door to work on somebody else's car. Or fix somebody else's plumbing. Or damaged roof.

The handiest of handymen, Travis' father was in high demand, making a decent living. At least by Green Hills standards. His hard work put food on the table and clothes on their backs. But there wasn't much left at the end of the month.

"A father wants more for his son. Getting a college education will give you a step up I never had."

"Baseball is my future. Why waste my time in school when I could be earning some money while I play?"

Absently, Travis ran a hand through his thick, dark hair. The tendency for the ends to curl came from his mother. As did his clear-blue eyes, straight nose, and the slight dent in the middle of his chin. She'd been a striking woman, her looks more arresting than beautiful.

On Travis, the combination wide-set eyes, strong jaw, and the tall, solid build so like his father's, was just the right mix that made girls sigh. He knew the effect he had on the opposite sex. And wasn't averse to using the fact to his advantage.

He's been blessed with a combination of good genes. Add a dash of his own innate charm. Girls liked him. He liked girls. End of story.

However, at the moment, Travis wasn't thinking about the opposite sex. He closed his eyes, counted to ten, and listened as his father recited the same old argument.

"A few bucks and no guarantee." Alan hefted the toolbox into the back of his twenty-year-old Ford. "The University of Kentucky has offered you a full-ride scholarship. Four years, Travis. From there, your chances of making it to the majors are better than starting out in single A ball."

"But—"

"What if you get injured? Or simply flame out?"

Travis snorted. His father always brought up a series of *what ifs*. Well, he had a few of his own.

"What if the world ends in the next six months? I'd rather spend the time playing pro-ball than worrying about passing Ms. Claymore's advanced calculus final."

"The world isn't going anywhere." Alan shot Travis a querying look. "Are you worried?"

His father knew the answer. The only thing Travis was better at than baseball was math. Both came as easy as breathing. However, he couldn't imagine spending his life solving equations.

Since the first time Travis slipped on a leather glove, his head was filled with images of scooping up grounders and hitting home runs. He constantly worked to get better, never content with local accolades.

Travis wanted to be the best. Period. Nothing would stand in his way. Not even a slew of *what-ifs*.

College was out. Travis knew he'd be drafted right out of high school. So what if the money wouldn't be great to start? He didn't doubt for a second that in a few years, he'd get his chance at a big contract.

Even through the haze of ambition and youthful arrogance, part of him understood his father's concerns. Out of love and respect, Travis could wait a little longer to follow his dreams.

"I'll turn down the offer to play winter ball."

"Thank you. And college? Will you at least keep an open mind?"

"Do you want me to lie?"

Laughing, Alan gave Travis an affectionate slap on the back.

"A lot can change in six months. Let your old man hold onto an ounce of hope. Okay?"

"An ounce? Sure, Dad." With a wave, Travis headed to school. "See you for dinner."

Travis wished he could give his father more. Their family consisted of just the two of them. His mother died when he was too young to remember. Like with every other obstacle put in his way, Alan Forsythe moved on. He persevered without the love of his life to help celebrate the good times and make the hard ones a little easier to bear.

Though they never spoke of the loss, Travis knew his father felt that part of him was missing. He worked harder, longer hours to fill the void. Dated, but never seemed interested in anything permanent.

Through everything, he never lost sight of his son, putting Travis and his needs first.

If college could have helped him get what he wanted—a long, successful, major league career—Travis wouldn't have hesitated. He liked learning. However, he'd never been fond of school. Continuing his education would be a lot more fun if he taught himself. Read the books that interested him. Studied only the subjects that caught his eye.

The idea that athletes were stupid muscle heads was a myth. Sure, there were always a few dumb jocks to be found. But not him.

Not Travis Forsythe. He planned to make his father proud. On and off the field.

Travis legged the two miles to the high school with ease, cutting through alleyways he knew like the back of his hand. Normally, he'd take his motorcycle. Unfortunately, the motor had started making an odd coughing sound on the way home yesterday.

Probably clogged spark plugs—a common problem with the temperamental machine. Travis loved his old bike. But if he calculated the time he actually spent riding the machine and how many hours tinkering with various parts, he knew the winning total would skew heavily toward the latter.

Scrapping the motorcycle would be the smart thing to do. However, Travis believed a man had the right to be stupid every now and then—as long as he was the only one affected.

Besides, trying to keep the heap of metal running kept Travis out of trouble.

Case in point. Last month, a group of his friends had their butts hauled into jail over in the neighboring town of Preston for disorderly conduct and underage drinking. Travis should have been with them. Instead, he was elbow deep in motor oil.

Eddie Hayes—Travis' best friend since they were old enough to crawl around in his family's backyard sandbox—accused him of turning into a boring, old man. Cursed with carrot-bright red hair, the freckles to match and a medium build that tended to run toward chubby, he'd always been the class clown. Cute more than handsome, he figured if he couldn't attract the girls with his good looks, he'd win them over with laughter.

A theory that seemed to work. Janey Moss, Eddie's current girlfriend, had a smile on her face more often than not.

"Teenagers are supposed to get in trouble," Eddie had explained as he recounted his two harrowing hours behind bars. "We raised a little hell. And you missed all the fun."

"You broke a plate-glass window, dented a police car, and will spend the next year working after school to repay your parents."

"Worth every dime." But Eddie didn't look as cocky as when he started his story of youthful rebellion.

"And the community service? Picking up garbage along the interstate?"

"Overreaction," Eddie muttered. "We'll survive. Plus, our reps are secured."

"Rebels *with* a cause," Travis snorted. "Nothing cooler than those reflective nylon vests they make you wear on road crew duty. Be sure and take a picture for posterity."

"Asshole."

In a way, Eddie had been right, Travis thought, picking up his pace as he passed an empty store along Main Street. He'd curbed most of his wild ways. A year ago, he would have led his friends.

Front of the pack. Drunk and disorderly—with relish.

Chet Fields, Green Hills' baseball coach, was the one who set Travis on a different path. As a man who had flirted with a career as a major league pitcher, his opinion held more weight than say, a teacher. Or even Travis' father.

Talent only counted for so much. To survive—to thrive—a player needed the right mindset. Scouts, managers, owners. They looked at more than batting average and fielding percentage.

They wanted leaders in the clubhouse. Not just the kind who made speeches, pumping up a locker room. But more important, men who set an example. Backed up their words with action.

Travis wasn't perfect. He struggled with the desire to raise hell with his friends—especially when they ragged on him—and the knowledge his coach was right.

Millions of kids played little league and high school ball. Only a handful had the chops to make the jump to the next level. Getting to the show? The big club? The major leagues? Not just making the leap, but staying there?

The odds against him were astronomical. Travis and his mad math skills could solve the equation in a flash and, if he were anybody else, the answer would have sent his nerves jangling into overdrive.

However, when baseball was involved, Travis was about as smooth an operator as there was. Not cocky—exactly. He knew he still had things to learn and never shirked the chance to put in the time and effort necessary.

Nerves and over-confidence were two different animals. When Travis slipped on his glove, stepping onto the field, everything was right with the world. He knew he belonged. He was home.

"Nothing wrong with a little arrogance," Coach Fields told him. "But never lose a trace of humility. Once you start to believe you can do no wrong, you will. I've seen more than one guy who was touted as the next big thing fall on his ass. Fast."

"Injuries?"

Travis swallowed hard at the thought. He—all athletes—tried not to think about his body betraying him. No matter how hard he worked. No matter how many hours he dedicated to becoming the best. One bad break could end his career in a snap.

"Sometimes," Coach nodded. Shaking his head, he ran a hand through his thinning, salt-and-pepper hair. "I know this isn't what you want to hear, Travis. But sometimes good—even great—isn't enough. For whatever reason, some phenoms do their damnedest, but the brass ring stays just out of their grasp."

Travis heard the words. Took them to heart. Then did what anybody with a dream had to do. He filed the advice away—way, way back in the recesses of his mind.

Nothing would stand in Travis' way. He couldn't see the future—what would be the fun in that? But he knew where he'd be in ten years. Playing ball. In the show.

"Well, what do we have here?"

As Travis passed the alley on the far side of the high school, he stopped in his tracks. He knew the owner of the taunting voice. Pete Doran was a bully. He liked nothing better than to torment someone weaker—always backed up by the group of sycophants who had been hanging off his coattails since first grade.

Like most bullies, under a layer of nasty swagger was a coward who never took on anybody able to fight back. One punch to the nose—delivered by Travis when they were twelve years old—was enough to keep Pete in check during school hours.

Most kids were smart enough to travel in packs. But occasionally—like now—Pete caught somebody alone.

Travis wasn't in the mood to play the hero. However, he couldn't walk away. With a sigh, he hung a sharp right.

"Why don't you lift up that sack you call a dress and let us see what you're hiding underneath?"

Jesus. Travis picked up his pace. Pete possessed little conscience when choosing a victim. His only criteria were that they were weaker and vulnerable. However, he wasn't known for going after girls. He must really be jonesing bad for his bully fix.

Surrounded by a half-dozen scruffy cohorts, Pete smugly took a bite from an apple. Blocked from his view, Travis couldn't see the person trapped against the wall of an old storage shed.

Imagining the girl scared. Undoubtedly crying. Unsure what was about to happen to her. Travis felt his blood start to boil.

"She's not arguing," Miles Weller—Pete's right-hand man— chuckled nastily. "I think she wants to give us a show."

Sick bastards. Travis shoved Miles aside—hard enough to send him toppling into Pete. The only thing that kept the goons on their feet was Pete's considerable bulk.

Simple physics. A hundred and forty pounds of skinny was no match for three hundred pounds of blubber.

"What the hell?" Pete's head whipped around, ready to eviscerate whoever dared interrupt his fun.

"My thoughts exactly. What the hell, Pete?"

Fear flitted through Pete's eyes. Along with frustration. And a big dose of hatred. Travis was just fine with all three.

"Get off." Pete pushed his so-called friend, sending Miles face first into the ground. "We was just havin' a little fun, Forsythe. What do you care what happens to Dippy Delaney? Nobody else does."

As Travis angled his body between Pete and his intended victim, he glanced at the girl. Delaney Pope. So quiet and unobtrusive. She always dressed in clothes three times too big. Wore old, scuffed loafers and ankle socks—the kind with incongruous lace trim around the folded over cuffs.

Long, dark hair—an indeterminate brown color—pulled back into a ponytail. Thick, black-rimmed glasses shielded her eyes—though she never looked up long enough from staring at the ground for a person to get a good look if he wanted to.

Delaney was meek. Quiet. A girl who had no friends to speak of. In other words, an easy mark for a bully on the prowl. Too easy. Even for an asshole like Pete Doran.

Expecting to see Delaney in tears—scared witless—Travis looked closer. Yes, she was afraid. Only a fool wouldn't be. But there were no tears filling her eyes. Only a sense of resignation.

Travis hated to see a girl cry, his gut twisting in helplessness every time. But Delaney's *been there, done that, what else is new* demeanor sent a chill down his spine. Somebody so young should be filled with hope.

Travis didn't know why, but he had the feeling Delaney had lost all hope a long time ago.

"Fun's over. Move along, assholes." Travis crossed his arms, feet planted firmly in front of the girl.

"Fuck you, Travis."

"Not in this lifetime. Or any other."

Travis could practically see Pete bite his tongue, holding back the words he didn't have the balls to speak. Red-faced, he turned, stomping off, his motley crew right on his heels.

"You okay?" Travis asked.

Delaney nodded. When Travis would have helped her straighten, she quickly tucked her hands behind her back, out of his reach.

Travis didn't push the issue, but damn. Skittish didn't begin to describe the girl.

"Pete shouldn't bother you again," Travis assured Delaney. "If he does, let me know. But in the future, try to avoid walking through alleys."

Delaney mumbled a response, so low Travis couldn't hear.

"Excuse me?"

"I didn't want to be late."

Travis glanced at this watch. If they hustled, they would beat the bell by a few minutes. He hadn't expected Delaney to fall at his feet in gratitude. But a simple thank you would have been nice.

Shaking his head, Travis picked up Delaney's dropped books. She hesitated, taking them, careful her fingers didn't come in contact with his. She wrapped her arms around the items—copies of advanced physics and ancient history—hunching her shoulders. She pushed her glasses up the bridge of her nose without giving Travis even a furtive glance. Shoulders hunched, she made her way toward the school, her stride short but fast.

Strange girl, Travis thought, trailing behind. Not too close, but close enough. Just in case Pete was dumber than the glob of jelly he resembled.

Travis had never given Delaney Pope much consideration. She was younger than the rest of his class. Sixteen maybe? The powers that be jumped her several grades just before they started their freshman year.

Four years walking the same halls. Taking many of the same classes. But for the life of him, Travis couldn't recall them exchanging a single word. Delaney slunk—an accurate description—through school, garnering less attention than a shadow.

The girl kept to herself. Quiet. Unseen.

Yet—obviously—Delaney Pope was smarter than the average teenager.

Intrigued in spite of himself, Travis watched as Delaney crossed the crowded parking lot. As she reached the sidewalk, she paused for a moment, then turned. Her knuckles were white, the grip on her books growing tighter.

"Watch out," she cried.

Instinct saved Travis. And phenomenal reflexes. He spun around, his hand snagging the half-eaten apple inches from smashing him in the side of the face. The fact that the damage would have been minimal didn't lessen his anger.

"You better run," Travis bit out. "If you ever try that again, you'll have the apple so far up your ass you'll be lucky if you ever shit the thing out."

Pete froze like a deer caught in the headlights. Before Travis could do more than fake a move in his direction, Pete made a beeline for the high school, moving faster than he had in his entire life.

"What a freaking wuss," Eddie Hayes said, grimacing at Pete's retreating figure. "If lard-ass hustled like that on the football field, he would have made all-state instead of Coach cutting him after one day."

"The only kind of exercise Pete believes in is the kind that gets him out of harm's way."

"The guy's stupid." Stating the obvious, Eddie chuckled. "But I never thought he was suicidal. What set him off?"

Travis shrugged, his gaze seeking out Delaney. He wasn't surprised to discover her nowhere to be found. He saved her. She returned the favor. The scales had readjusted to even.

Strange girl, Travis thought again. *Yet interesting*, he amended.

"Earth to Travis," Eddie snapped his fingers, regaining Travis' wandering attention. "Time for boring English."

"I like English."

"You like Ms. Oswald and her glorious array of clingy sweaters."

Forgetting Delaney with the ease of any hormonal teenager, Travis grinned when the image of Ms. Oswald's sizable breasts popped into his brain.

"I do love her... sweaters. Especially the fuzzy blue one."

Realizing he still held the offending apple, he sent the dripping piece of fruit arching toward the garbage can.

Whoosh. Nothing but net.

CHAPTER TWO

● ≈ ● ≈ ●

"WANT TO FOOL around in the shower?"

Travis suppressed a groan. Lorna Steele—dressed in her Green Hills Rangers cheerleading outfit brushed her hand across his sweaty chest. In Lorna speak, *fool around* meant no holds barred and don't forget the condom.

Lorna didn't care if other guys wandered in and out of the locker room. Or if any of them stopped to watch. The danger of getting caught was half the thrill.

After an hour in the weight room followed by five miles around the outdoor track, Travis wasn't interested in playing water games with Lorna. Or that was what he told himself. His body—led by his dick—had different ideas.

Down, boy, Travis cautioned.

Lorna acted as if she only wanted a good time. But if she had her way, when he left town, she'd go with him. The proverbial June bride. Orange blossoms danced in the cheerleader's head. Along with dreams of her life as a baseball superstar's pampered wife.

"Aren't you dating Duncan Cornwall?" Travis asked as he peeled Lorna's short, but sharp nails from around his wrist.

"Duncan is sweet," Lorna purred. "But I prefer a little more… meat on my man."

"Consider my *meat* off your personal menu, Lorna." Stopping at the locker room door, Travis blocked her entry. "Go play with somebody else. I'm not interested."

"You were last summer."

"We had fun."

"More than fun," Lorna insisted, used to getting what she wanted. "You said I was the best you ever had."

"Did I?" Honestly, Travis couldn't remember.

"Please, Travis?" Lorna pouted, her heavily mascara-coated eyelashes batting up a storm. Despite what she believed, the look wasn't a good one for her. "Once more? For old time's sake?"

Warning bells sounded in Travis' head. *Danger! Danger!* If this was her attempt at a trap, too bad. Whatever Lorna had planned, he didn't want to find out.

"I thought we were friends."

"We are," Lorna insisted.

"Then don't ruin some really good memories by doing something we'll both regret."

"But—"

"Go home, Lorna." Travis backed into the locker room. "Give Duncan a call. He's a good guy."

Duncan deserved better, but the guy was obviously smitten with Lorna. Setting him straight wasn't up to Travis.

As he opened his locker, Travis glanced at the shower. Why tempt fate? Or rely on Lorna to do the smart thing? Deciding to wait until he was in the safety of his own bathroom to clean up, he grabbed his jacket and headed out the back way.

Clouds filled the early evening sky, threatening rain. For once, Travis had his motorcycle in running order. If he was lucky, he'd be parked in the garage before the first drops hit the ground.

Travis was about to pull on his helmet when he paused, the faint sound of music reaching his ears. Cocking his head, he listened, trying to figure out the name of the song. His dad loved anything classical, playing his old records during dinner.

Without realizing his brain had been infiltrated, Travis had acquired an appreciation for the genre.

The music room at Green Hills High, located in a converted maintenance building, wasn't large. Or particularly well equipped. A dilapidated drum set. A few brass instruments that had long ago lost their luster. And one used, upright piano donated to the school so long ago nobody could remember the name of the generous benefactor.

Travis walked by the building almost every day on his way to the gym. But he'd never had a reason—or inclination—to enter the dented, metal, west-facing door. Turning the handle, he supposed curiosity was as good a motivator as any.

The room was dark, the only light coming from a small gooseneck lamp sitting on the top of the old piano. The piano sat in the far corner of the small, rectangular room.

At the piano, hunched over in what seemed to be her natural position, sat Delaney Pope.

Travis had expected to find Mr. Leech, the science/music teacher. Or perhaps Marianne Rogers, the only student he knew for a fact played the piano on a regular basis. There were dozens of people he would have expected to see, fingers running expertly over the keys, other than Delaney Pope.

How could such a quiet, introverted little mouse play with so much emotion? How could she hide this part of her so thoroughly? The feeling she put into every note.

Who could have guessed that all this passion lay hidden under a tent-like dress and sensible shoes?

Afraid to break the spell, Travis gently closed the door. Slowly—careful to keep Delaney's back to him—he moved further into the room. The soles of his sneakers made no sound on the linoleum floor, allowing him to close the distance without disturbing her concentration.

Though Travis doubted Delaney would have noticed if the building began crumbling around her. She was in a world all her own. A zone that he recognized from when he was at home plate, a bat in his hands, his mind totally focused on one thing. Hitting the ball into the gap. Or out of the park. Anywhere the defense wasn't.

Sometimes—more often than not—when Travis focused, he could shut out everything around him. The sound of the crowd disappeared. The taunts from the opposing catcher were useless. Even the calls from the umpire were muffled. Nothing existed except him and the pitcher. A one-on-one battle that, more often than not, Travis won. Handily.

Who would have guessed? Watching Delaney, Travis felt a surprising tug. A connection. A new understanding—on some level—of who she was and what made her tick.

The music helped. Travis stopped a few feet away, closing his eyes, processing exactly how the melody made him feel.

Sad was the first word that came to mind. But sadness was only the surface. A little deeper, he encountered wistfulness. Travis wanted to believe hope might lurk somewhere in the piece—he couldn't say.

Suddenly, as Delaney's hands finally stilled, Travis understood. Each note. Each passage. They would stay with him long after tonight. Part her, part something elusive. Hauntingly beautiful.

All leading to a question Travis had to ask.

"Who wrote that?"

Delaney jumped, her only sound a muted gasp. Spinning around, her eyes wide, she blinked several times before her hand went to her face, feeling for something that wasn't there.

"You aren't wearing your glasses."

Travis knew he'd stated the obvious. But he couldn't help himself. He'd never seen Delaney without the dark rims. She turned her face away, fumbling, her hand knocked the glasses onto the floor.

Kneeling, Travis retrieved the frames, holding the lens up to the light to check for any damage.

"What the—?"

Looking closer, Travis couldn't believe what he saw.

"Please." Delaney's hands twisted in her lap, a frown of distress on her diverted face. "I need those."

"No, you don't." Travis folded the glasses, setting them on the piano, well within Delaney's reach. "Those lenses are nothing but clear glass. Why bother?"

Caught out, Delaney's head hung lower, but she didn't speak.

"Talk to me. I promise I won't bite, Del."

"What did you call me?" Delaney asked, her chin lifting just enough so her gaze hit Travis mid-chest.

"Del? Do you prefer Delaney?"

"No. I—" Travis had to lean closer to hear her barely whispered words. "My father used to call me Del. Everybody else calls me Laney."

"You don't like Laney?"

Delaney shrugged. "I've heard worse."

Children could be cruel—especially when they perceived somebody as different. Bullies like Pete Doran used his physical superiority to lash out. But words could be just as hurtful. More so.

Travis felt a surge of protectiveness and a smattering of guilt. He'd never made an effort to befriend Delaney. Never given her a smile. Or spoken a kind word. Didn't that make him responsible? At least on some level?

"I'm sorry."

"Why?"

"For not seeing you before now."

Slowly, Delaney raised her head, her gaze wide with surprise. Travis looked into her eyes and felt as if somebody punched him in the gut—every ounce of breath rushing from his lungs.

Purple, he thought with wonder. The color of Delaney's irises was like jewels. Precious and rare. Why would she hide them behind a pair of ugly, unnecessary glasses?

"I have to go," Delaney broke the spell, fumbling to return the glasses to their usual place on her nose, masking her amazing eyes. Done, she jumped to her feet.

"Wait."

Travis grabbed her arm, and all hell broke loose. At least, Delaney's version of hell.

"Don't," she shrieked, violently pulling from his grip.

The momentum of the move caused Delaney to stumble, her feet tangling, her legs twisting. Travis reached for her, hoping to stop her fall, but his attempt to help only made things worse.

Delaney—seemingly more afraid of Travis' touch than hitting the floor—jerked her body to the left. As a result, instead of landing on her backside, she crashed hard into a group of music stands.

Helpless to prevent the disaster, Travis watched as Delaney landed in a painful heap, her legs and arms twisted at odd angles. But the worst was the sound of her head hitting the floor where, under the linoleum, lay nothing but unforgiving cement.

The dull thud made Travis wince.

"Stay where you are," Travis cautioned.

Delaney didn't listen, scrambling to sit up. Travis would have held her down, knowing if she was injured moving would be a huge mistake. But he was afraid of her reaction. One touch from him might make a bad situation worse.

"Home." Glasses askew, hair falling around her face, Delaney rose to her feet with the grace of a newborn colt. "I'm late. Can't be late."

For the second time in less than a week, Travis found himself trailing Delaney. Not too close—like the last time. He wasn't worried about a lurking bully. Instead, he was scared to death she was about to fall flat on her face.

"At least let me give you a ride."

"No!"

The panic in Delaney's voice did nothing to allay Travis' fears.

"Great," he sighed as they left the music room. The rain was no longer a threat. The skies had opened up. They were in the middle of a deluge. "My bike won't keep you dry, but at least I'll get you home before you drown."

Delaney didn't answer. She simply lowered her head and ran.

"Maybe she isn't as strange as I thought," Travis grumbled to himself, straddling his bike. "But something weird is going on."

Crazy? Travis dismissed the idea, revving the engine. The strap on his helmet firmly secured under his chin, he headed after Delaney. Trailing her was getting to be a way of life. Before it became a habit, he wanted some answers.

Travis knew a lot of girls and not one of them complained when he touched them. Just the opposite.

Maybe Delaney *was* a little touched in the head. A lot of geniuses were. He offered a helping hand. Pure and simple. What does she do? She acted as if he was after her virtue.

Travis snorted. Delaney Pope should be so lucky. Stunning purple eyes aside, that girl wasn't his type.

Following Delaney was easy enough—wet, but easy. She didn't take any shortcuts, staying on the main road. Travis kept the bike's headlight trained on her, almost stopping when she tripped, landing on her knees. But she scrambled to her feet, barreling on through the unrelenting rain before he could pull over.

Five minutes into their less than enjoyable adventure, Delaney turned onto Helton Street. The families who lived in this neighborhood weren't poor. Or wealthy. Closer to middle class—barely. Houses of the same design—not too big, not too small—built in neat little rows. Affordable, not fancy.

Delaney opened the gate of the third house on the right, the small, curtained, front window lit from within. In a few steps, she was on the porch.

"You're welcome," Travis yelled above the sound of his bike and the pouring rain.

Without a backward glance, Delaney disappeared through the door.

The girl really needed to learn how to say thank you.

Laughing at himself, Travis wondered if he was the crazy one. Delaney hadn't needed him. She made her way home safe and sound without his help. If she caught pneumonia, that was her problem. If he caught the malady, he had nobody to blame but himself.

Making a loop, Travis paused the bike at the stop sign, trying without much success to wipe the water from his helmet's visor. A fool's errand from start to finish.

Hitting the gas, Travis finally headed home.

Yeah. Crazy sounded about right.

CHAPTER THREE

● ≈ ● ≈ ●

"LAST NIGHT CAN never happen again, Laney," Alma Brill whispered.

She always kept her voice at the same low, barely there level whether her husband was in the house or not. The less attention she drew to herself the better. A lesson she'd learned the hard way.

"Good thing Munch wasn't home when you got here."

Delaney poked at the bowl of oatmeal—thick and lumpy and totally unappetizing—keeping her head down. The only time they could breathe was when Munch wasn't around. Even then, they lived in fear, looking at the clock. Wondering when he'd walk through the door. Lord and master.

More like a jailer. There were no bars on the windows but make no mistake. This house was a prison.

Delaney wished she had the nerve—the backbone—to stand up and protest. She was so tired of walking on eggshells. Tired of suppressing every thought. Sick and tired of hiding her true self. Or rather, who she used to be.

Happy. Full of life. Eager to see what new adventure life had in store.

Did that girl still exist? She didn't know. Not anymore. God, she hoped so. But she'd never find out locked inside the walls she had—from necessity—built around herself.

Seven years. Ever since Henry, call me Munch, Brill had come into their lives. A whirlwind romance and suddenly Alma Pope had a new husband. And Delaney, a stepfather.

In his late thirties, he was a man of average height, but powerful, with thick muscles and a handsome face. Thick, dark hair and dark eyes. At first, Munch seemed like a dream. Until— with the flip of an invisible switch—he turned into their worst nightmare.

Bright beyond her years, Delaney still longed for a father figure, someone to replace the man who disappeared from her life—first through divorce, then, a year later, when he died in a car accident. Delaney's mother wanted to feel wanted by a man.

The Popes—mother and daughter—welcomed Munch with open arms. Munch, once Alma and Delaney were moved into his home, revealed his true self.

A controlling bully. A drinker. An abuser. More than once, Alma would hide from the world until the bruise on her face faded enough to hide with strategically applied makeup.

And—though Delaney didn't understand at the time—Munch Brill turned out to be a man with no compunction about grooming his stepdaughter to one day share his bed.

During the first few years, Munch showed his affection in ways that wouldn't raise any red flags. Hugs mostly. A few quick kisses—always on the mouth. Delaney didn't feel anything was wrong. Why would she? Why would she balk when he insisted she sit on his lap while they watched television after dinner?

She was his favorite little girl.

How Delaney had grown to hate that phrase. She hated the way Munch would tuck her into bed at night, the thin cotton nightgown no protection as his big, rough hands brushed against her vulnerable, budding body.

And the way Munch would lean close, to brush a kiss across her lips. The smell of his breath—rank with stale whiskey— making her stomach turn.

Seven long years. Delaney couldn't pinpoint the exact moment she knew something wasn't right. When she figured out Munch's *so-called affections* weren't normal. However, ever since, she lived in dread. When would he move beyond the leering looks? When would he grow tired of sickening bedtime touches and wet-lipped pecks?

Delaney knew the day was coming. And soon. Munch seemed fixated on her next birthday. June tenth. Six months from today.

Sweet sixteen and never been kissed.

Not a real, honest to goodness, man/woman kiss. Munch always grinned when he said the words. And winked. As if he carried a secret that he'd soon share only with her.

Munch considered Delaney to be his. And made certain boys stayed away. The baggy dresses and thick glasses materialized long before the emergence of her body's first curve.

"Keep your head down and your smiles to yourself." Munch spent the entire summer after he married her mother indoctrinating Delaney into the way she was expected to act from now on.

"Boys only want one thing. Since you'll never give it to them, no point in getting their hopes up. Right?"

Delaney was too young, too innocent to know what Munch meant. But she learned. Not from the boys in her class. But from the man who—in theory—was supposed to keep her safe.

Delaney shuddered again, this time drawing her mother's attention.

"Aren't you feeling well?" Alma put a cool hand to Delaney's forehead. "Did you catch a cold walking home in the rain?"

"People don't get sick from a little rain, Mom."

"Are you sure?" Alma frowned, checking Delaney's throat for swollen glands."

"Old wives' tale."

"So smart," Alma touched Delaney's cheek, a brief wisp of pride coloring the typically dull gray of her eyes. "However, since I'm an old wife, cut me some slack. Stick out your tongue."

Rather than argue, she did as directed. As her mother peered into her mouth, Delaney sighed.

In truth, Alma Brill *was* a wife, but she wasn't old. The lines around her mouth, the dark circles under eyes. They weren't from the passage of time, but from living a downtrodden, stress-ridden existence. One of her own making.

Leaving wasn't possible. Alma tried. Taking Delaney, she headed out of town. They didn't get far. And the price she paid—a broken arm and two missing teeth—was nothing compared to what Munch told her he'd do if she ever tried it again. He'd never raised a hand to Delaney. But he could. Yes, he could.

The arm healed. The teeth were replaced. But Alma never forgot. Munch never let her.

Any fight left in her mother was gone. In seven long, unrelenting years, she'd become a shell of her former self. A thin, cowed, timid shell. And Delaney—had followed suit.

Like herself, Delaney could barely remember Alma any other way. She tried to picture her mother's smile but came up blank. God, how sad was that?

Who are you? Delaney wondered as her mother went back to scrubbing the kitchen counter. Who am I?

Losing herself was the most frightening part. Most of the time, Delaney felt invisible. Her classmates looked right through her. Or—if one of them took the time to notice—they ridiculed her. Called her names. Cornered her in an alley intent on…

Delaney would never know how far Pete Doran and his goon squad might have gone if Travis Forsythe hadn't intervened. And she was grateful. Truly.

However—for some unfathomable reason—she also felt a spark of resentment that the great hero-worshiped athlete would deign to come off his pedestal long enough to help poor Delaney Pope.

Some girls—the ones she heard giggling in the halls—would have swooned just at the thought of Travis coming to their rescue. Delaney wasn't one of them.

And then he had to intrude on the only thing that made her happy. The one part of her life she had to look forward to.

Her music. Her sanctuary.

Travis Forsythe might charm the rest of the student body with his smile, but Delaney wanted him to leave her alone. When he'd looked at her—really looked—she felt an odd rush through her blood she couldn't explain. And didn't want to analyze.

For what seemed like forever, Delaney wished for someone to realize she wasn't simply a shadow that flitted unnoticed along the periphery of their life. She dreamed of finding a friend. That person was not—could not be—Travis.

Even if Travis was interested—which was so far beyond the realm of likely, Delaney wondered why she bothered to speculate—Munch would have a fit if a boy started hanging around.

A long-forgotten flicker of rebellion tried to push past Delaney's hopelessness, only to be snuffed out when her mother set a brown paper bag on the table.

"Here's your lunch, Laney. And remember. Munch will be home early today. So, don't dawdle after school."

Delaney took the bag—the same kind she took to school day after day. Year after year. Plain, boring. Inside and out. Just like her.

A boy like Travis Forsythe could shape his own future. The possibilities were limitless.

A girl like Delaney Pope?

Something had to change—and soon—or she wouldn't have a future. Delaney's options were few. If she left, Alma would pay the price. Unfortunately, convincing her mother to run again wouldn't be easy.

She could submit. Just the thought made the vomit rise in the throat. Delaney swallowed. Or...? She'd always stopped before she let herself finish the sentence. Once she did, she knew she couldn't take the thought back.

Delaney hoped, when the time came, she had the nerve to do what she had to do. Escape wasn't possible. Submission, unthinkable.

But death? Maybe.

Rising, she picked up her books and paper bag, telling her mother goodbye.

A welcome calm settled over Delaney. If she was given no other choice? Yes. She could live with death.

CHAPTER FOUR

● ≈ ● ≈ ●

"WHAT'S WITH YOU today?" Eddie asked, shoving Travis along in the lunch line. "I don't know if your head is in the clouds or up your ass."

"Watch the language, Mr. Hayes."

"Sorry, Ms. Perkins," Eddie muttered at their English teacher's reminder of the school's strict no-cursing policy. "The woman is halfway across the cafeteria. How could she hear me?"

"Bat ears," Travis said, keeping his back to Ms. Perkins. "Or she read your lips."

"You think?" Just in case, Eddie put his hand over his mouth as a shield.

"Her son is deaf. Maybe she learned."

"Too bad about her kid. But I call unfair advantage."

Travis hid his grin. Truth was, Ms. Perkins didn't have any children. But he loved yanking Eddie's chain.

"Students outnumber teachers. By a large number. How can you begrudge the woman a little something to help even the playing field?"

"In theory, I can't. But she has the power. My permanent record is at Ms. Perkin's mercy."

Eyes on the cafeteria door, Travis' gaze sharpened when Delaney Pope entered. Finally. He tracked her progress, noticing the way she almost hugged the wall, head down, clutching a book to her chest with one hand, a brown paper bag with the other.

"By now, your permanent record is what it is," Travis said absently, frowning when Delaney took a seat at an empty table. "Why start worrying now?"

"According to the guidance counselor, my chances of getting into the University of Washington are borderline. The red marks in my file for untoward behavior—her words, not mine—could be the difference. I blame Perkins."

Travis picked up a tray, loading on a fork, knife, spoon, three napkins, and two cartons of milk.

"I blame your uncontrollable need to pull practical jokes."

Eddie grinned, his tray mirroring Travis'.

"Filling Principal York's office with chickens was pure genius. An all-time classic. Kids will be talking about that one for generations. And I would've gotten away scot-free if Randy Simmons had kept his mouth shut."

"Three days suspension and two days cleaning chicken shit off every inch of the office. Plus, the weekend you lost repainting the walls."

"I don't know what old man Stoneridge fed those birds, but sometimes I swear I can still smell the stuff they crapped out. Who knew chickens could suffer from diarrhea?" Eddie shuddered at the memory.

Smiling, Travis nodded at the lady behind the counter. Mrs. Muir had worked at the school since long before he was born. She arrived early every morning, tucking her cap of silver hair into a perfunctory protective net. Donning a starched white apron.

The thirty extra pounds she carried on her five-foot-nothing frame meshed perfectly with her perpetually affable, everybody's granny, demeanor.

However, make no mistake. Sweet could turn to iron-fisted in a flash. After forty years, she was the last person to put up with teenage antics. Mess around while standing in her lunch line, and she pounced like a hungry lion after a defenseless lamb.

Because the students liked her—and because they were more than a little intimidated by a mere lift of her brow—the lunch room was the best behaved, no drama area in the entire school.

"Hamburgers and tater tots," Eddie sighed with pleasure. "My favorite day of the month. Hey, where are you going?"

Instead of taking a right toward their usual table—the one they and their crowd had occupied every day without fail since freshman year—Travis turned left. An impulse. Unexplainable, even to himself.

"I'll see you in class."

"But—"

"Later," Travis said with a wave.

Eddie watched for a few seconds as Travis weaved around the tables, then with a shrug, continued on, more interested in his stomach than his friend's odd behavior.

As he walked, Travis wondered what he was doing. Why he'd developed a sudden interest in the habits of Delaney Pope.

He thought he'd put her from his thoughts.

After driving home and taking a much-needed, long, hot shower, Travis enjoyed dinner with his father, followed by an hour of television before finishing up a term paper for history class.

Admittedly, Delaney flitted through his thoughts once or twice. Why wouldn't she? After their meeting in the music room, followed by the way she rushed home—with him foolishly following behind—he was bound to wonder about her just a little.

However, by morning, Travis was more worried about the fact that his motorcycle wouldn't start—as usual. As he grumbled all the way to school, Delaney, and her odd behavior—didn't cross his mind.

Until he caught a glimpse of her in the hall.

Dressed in her usual baggy dress—dark green today—scuffed loafers and ankle socks, she occupied the same unremarkable space as always. As close to invisible as a person could be. Yet today,

Travis zeroed in on her immediately, as if she was suddenly painted bright red neon.

Delaney couldn't go back to hiding. Not from him.

Travis had heard her play the piano. So intensely beautiful, the notes still resonated through his brain. He knew what she hid behind those incongruously thick, completely unnecessary, black-rimmed glasses.

Shy he could understand. But Delaney's problem went far beyond the simple malady. Travis had the feeling—if humanly possible—she'd welcome the oblivion of total nothingness.

Why? Delaney was intelligent beyond the scope of his understanding. She had musical talent—a gross understatement. And, she was pretty. Now that Travis took the time to look, he knew she had more to offer than just a pair of stunning purple eyes.

Who was Delaney Pope? What was her story? Travis knew himself. Now that she was on his radar, he wouldn't be happy until he knew the answers.

Stopping by the table where Delaney sat alone, nibbling on a sandwich while engrossed in her book, Travis set down his tray.

"Mind if I join you?"

Delaney gasped, her head shooting up, her glasses tilting to the side. In one motion, she lowered her head, fixed her glasses, and frowned.

"What are you doing?" she hissed.

"I'm about to eat my lunch." He slid onto the bench seat, opposite Delaney. "With you. Any objection?"

Her eyes, what Travis could see of them, quickly moved from side to side, looking for God knows what. If possible, she sunk further into herself, her shoulders rounding into an uncomfortable looking ball.

"Go away. Please."

"Nope." Travis popped a tot into his mouth. "I like where I am."

"Why?" Delaney asked, her tone almost desperate.

"I've never eaten lunch over here. I decided getting a new perspective might be a good thing." Travis slowly surveyed the room. "I was right."

"Fine. If you won't go, I will."

Delaney smashed her sandwich into the crumpled bag. Swinging her legs around, she banged her knee. Hard. Travis winced in sympathy.

"Careful."

The look Delaney shot him—filled with frustration and just enough anger to make Travis smile—gave him a glimmer of hope. Perhaps under all the cowering lurked a trace of a backbone.

"Fine," Travis sighed dramatically. "If you would rather eat outside, I don't mind. But I think we're due for some more rain."

To no surprise, Delaney didn't answer. Instead, her eyes widened in what he hoped was exasperation before she scurried for the exit. Picking up his tray, he followed.

"You lead, I follow," he called out, garnering the attention of half the room. Whispered gossip flew from table to table, ensuring that by the time he reached the door, every person in the room knew he was about to leave—and why.

Travis caught up with Delaney, holding the door for her.

"Chasing women isn't my usual style. But what the heck. Just this once."

Delaney rushed around the corner to a place where nobody could see them. She didn't raise her voice, but her head shot up in a flash, giving Travis his first look at her face in the light of day.

Oh, yes, he thought, taking in the flush of red that stained her cheeks. Pretty. If she made a little effort to stand up straight, and maybe smile now and then? Who knew? Beautiful wasn't out of the realm of possibility.

"I asked you to leave me alone."

"Yes," Travis nodded slowly. "I believe you did."

"Then, why didn't you?"

"I'd like to be your friend."

Travis didn't know who was more surprised by his declaration. Delaney, or him? She was a mystery that needed solving. Nothing more. Besides, he had all the friends he needed. Why should he push himself on a girl who didn't want any part of him?

The flash of want—ever so brief—on her face gave Travis his answer. He'd never met anybody who needed a friend more than Delaney.

"You—" Delaney swallowed. Her eyes narrowed. "Are you trying to make me the butt of a joke the whole school—besides me—is in on?"

"Jesus. Really?" Travis shook his head. "You've watched too many bad teenage comedies."

"I haven't been to see a movie in forever."

"What about on television?"

Delaney shook her head.

A typical teenager, Travis couldn't imagine a life without TV. Or movies. The small theater in Green Hills was a little behind the times, but eventually, all the new releases made their way to town.

Rather than possibly making Delaney feel bad—Travis changed the subject back to where they started.

"What do you say? Friends?"

"I'm not a charity case."

"If you were, I wouldn't be interested." Travis' lips quirked, filled with self-deprecation. "I'm the least altruistic person you'll ever meet."

"Travis." Eddie rounded the corner. With long-practiced ease, he quickly dismissed Delaney with little more than a glance. "The whole school is buzzing. What the hell is going on?"

"Can't you see I'm busy?"

"With her?"

Delaney took her chance, brushing past Travis. Her book hit his arm, falling to the ground. She hesitated, her eyes filled with longing, but gave up, leaving the pieces of bound paper where they lay—a kind of collateral damage.

"Delaney! Wait!"

Travis' entreaty fell on deaf ears. Before he could call out again, Delaney was safely out of his range, inside the school.

"Damn it."

"Spill, man." Eddie gave Travis a shove. "Why the interest in what's her name?"

"Her name is Delaney," Travis ground out.

"Whatever."

Two things kept Travis from plowing his fist into the sneer on Eddie's face. Years of friendship. And the fact that—before yesterday—Travis would have dismissed Delaney with equal ease.

The knowledge didn't sit well.

"Never mind." Travis slapped Eddie on the back—a little harder than necessary. "Let's get to class."

"Sure." With a frown, Eddie rubbed his shoulder. "Whatever you say."

Travis bent, picking up the book, absently checking the title, expecting some dull, non-fiction historical tome. However, what he found was as far from dull and dry as he could imagine, making him grin.

Passion Under a Moonlit Sky.

Delaney Pope read romance novels? Not only was the girl a mystery. She was—to Travis' growing puzzlement—full of surprises.

OUT OF BREATH, Delaney ran into the bathroom, locking herself in the stall as far away from the door as possible. At any second, she expected her heart to burst from her chest. Taking a seat, she filled her lungs. In. Out. In. Out.

All around Delaney, voices buzzed. Girls—fixing their hair, applying layer after layer of lip glass—exchanged nonsensical comments about boys, their current favorite band, or television show, or blouse. And then they returned to boys. First and foremost, boys ruled their conversations.

Delaney settled her feet on the toilet seat rim, her arms locked around her legs. These girls—her peers, her classmates—weren't interested in her or her problems. Perhaps if they knew what she hid behind the wall she'd built around herself. If they had any inkling that beyond the stooped shoulders and baggy dresses lay a girl in trouble, one or two of them might have reached out.

How to make the first move? Delaney didn't know. To them, she was the weird girl they had long ago ceased to notice.

Except somebody had noticed.

Travis Forsythe. One of the most popular boys in school wanted to be her friend? Why? What was his motive? And wouldn't those giggly girls who went on and on about him, their sighs almost rapturous, be amazed if they found out.

Resting her cheek on her knees, Delaney's lips curved ever so slightly. Travis Forsythe had asked to be her friend. Imagine. The impossible had come true.

For a brief moment, Delaney allowed herself to float on the possibility. Somebody to talk to. To confide in. She didn't want anything romantic, and she was certain Travis felt the same.

Friends. Delaney decided the word—and all it encompassed— was her favorite. Bar none.

As if somebody snapped her fingers, cruelly ending her wonderful dream, Delaney tumbled back to reality, her smile gone.

The giggly girls would never find out about Travis' offer. Nobody would. She couldn't have a friend—especially a boy. What if Munch found out? A shaft of fear raced down Delaney's spine, not for herself. For Travis.

When riled, Munch was unpredictable. Usually, he took his anger and frustration out on his wife, using Alma as his own private punching bag. However, on the occasions when he used his fists on somebody else, his family took care of any potential backlash.

His brother, Rick Brill, was the town sheriff. His uncle, Horace Detwiler, had been mayor for over twenty years. Plus, all the cousins and relatives by marriage wielded way too much power to be ignored—were better than a get out of jail free card.

Not once—for all his many crimes and misdeeds—had Munch been arrested. Or spent a single second behind bars.

The feeling of helplessness that permeated Delaney's existence had become a constant, unshakable companion. She hadn't given up all hope. But she was close.

One thing kept Delaney going. The college scholarships she'd applied for with the help of Ms. Watts. A roving counselor, once a month, she visited a dozen different schools—all too small to keep her on as a full-time employee.

Because Ms. Watts didn't live in Green Hills, she wasn't influenced by Munch and his family. Her only concern was her students.

More than once, Delaney had been tempted to unburden herself, but after keeping silent for so long, she didn't know where to start. The words would rise up in her throat, only to form a lump she couldn't push out.

Besides, what could the sweet but less than robust looking middle-aged woman have done? Other than make a bad situation worse.

Delaney getting away from Munch had dwindled with each passing year. Slim to none about summed up her chances. His family had a wide reach. As long as she was underage and legally bound to his control, running would be difficult.

Hiding? Almost impossible.

However, she did have one ace in the hole. A secret she needed to keep to herself as long as possible.

Ms. Watts seemed hopeful that Delaney could score a full-ride scholarship. Applications had been filled out. Sent with fingers, toes, and anything else she could cross.

California. Oregon. Washington. Even Alaska. Far, far away from South Carolina, Munch, and his many-tentacled family.

Hawaii was her dream. Delaney hugged herself tighter at the thought. Warm, sandy beaches would be nice. The freedom they represented even better.

Alma would be a problem. She couldn't leave her mother behind and trying to convince the meek shell of a woman to run would be almost impossible. But if the moment came—*please, please, please*—she was determined to figure out a way.

As for Travis? Delaney sighed.

Where had he been seven years ago? Even six? Back when she would have welcomed him as her friend. Before she was completely cowed by Munch and his sick obsession.

Maybe—with a friend like Travis—Delaney could have kept her identity. Or at least a bit of backbone. Maybe not. Either way, he was too late. She didn't want to risk Munch's wrath.

Delaney was tempted. However, she had herself and her mother to worry about. The last thing she needed was to be responsible for putting an innocent young man in her stepfather's crosshairs.

Travis would thank her if he knew. However, since she couldn't tell him, Delaney would do what she'd learned to do best.

Blend into the woodwork.

CHAPTER FIVE

● ≈ ● ≈ ●

DELANEY QUICKLY DISCOVERED that avoiding Travis Forsythe was harder than she could have imagined.

She'd become used to flying under people's radar. Days could go by without another student saying a word to her. Teachers—rather than fight a losing battle—had long ago stopped trying to get her to participate during class. Delaney did her assignments, received excellent grades. In fact, academically, she sat at the top of her class.

Socially, she was… nothing. Someday, Delaney promised herself, she'd push out of her shell. But not now. Not today. Or in the next six months. When she burst from her cocoon, she'd be far away from Green Hills.

Unfortunately, Travis had other ideas. Hard to avoid—sneaky. Why was he picking on her?

His campaign—Delaney couldn't think of any other way to describe Travis' tactics—began the next day.

"Good morning," Travis said with a warm smile.

Certain he couldn't be speaking to her, Delaney kept her head down as she took her books from her locker. The one on the end of the row—where she could get in and out with as little fuss and muss as possible.

"I said good morning, Del." Travis bent over just enough to bring his face even with hers. "Now, you say, good morning, Travis."

Delaney didn't know who was more surprised. The pretty brunette sophomore who—only a few feet to the right—had quite naturally assumed Travis had meant his greeting for her? Or Delaney, who wished she could crawl into her locker and lock the door?

Rather than stick around and contemplate the answer, Delaney scooted around the gaping girl—and several of her friends— careful not to look at Travis. She didn't know what had gotten into him, but whatever his problem, the last thing she wanted to do was give him any encouragement.

"See you in class."

Delaney bit her lip. Hard. But not because Travis' sudden interest upset her. Inexplicably—for the first time in she didn't know how long—she wanted to laugh.

Skirting around the crowd that always seemed to follow Travis from place to place, Delaney couldn't resist taking a peek, hoping he wouldn't notice. No such luck. As if reading her mind, he grinned. And winked.

Delaney concealed her laugh behind a cough. And people called *her* crazy.

Entering her first period advanced calculus class, she took her usual seat in the back. Travis always sat near the middle. Delaney waited, wondering if he'd break protocol and sit by her. To her relief—honestly, she assured herself, she *was* relieved—he barely glanced her way as he slid his long, lanky body onto the same chair he occupied every day.

Deciding Travis had his fun and would now leave her be, Delaney opened her book, immersing herself in the one part of her life that always made sense. She loved school. Thrived on learning.

English. History. Science. Math. She embraced them all, her mind a sponge, eagerly soaking up every bit of knowledge.

Advanced calculus was a highlight of her day. Though Delaney had little trouble with the curriculum, Ms. Bennett had the ability to make the subject interesting—at times, even challenging.

"The test on Friday will cover chapters six through ten," Ms. Bennett informed them just before the end of the class. "If you have any questions, let me know."

"Do you have any questions?" Travis whispered as they filed from the room, his voice low so only Delaney could hear.

"No." Delaney knew the smartest thing to do would be not to engage, but she found the reply passing her lips before she could remember to bite her tongue.

"Silly question. You always know the answers."

"No. I don't." Not about anything really important.

Travis fell in step with her, drawing the kind of attention Delaney had always succeeded in avoiding. Until now.

The popular jock and the invisible girl. The oddest of odd couples. Not that they were a couple. God forbid.

Delaney's thoughts raced as she tried to think of a way to get rid of Travis. She couldn't begin to guess where his thoughts ran.

"I would love to know what questions could possibly stump you," Travis said. "Another time. Want to eat lunch together?"

"No."

"I have practice after school, or I'd offer to walk you home. Maybe tomorrow?"

"No!"

Travis didn't seem to hear the horror in Delaney's voice. Or he chose to ignore it.

"Okay." Travis shrugged, obviously not the least bit concerned by her terse response. "See you later."

Dumbfounded, Delaney watched as Travis wound his way through the hall, answering as somebody called out to him. Nodding to his friends. Flirting with every girl as if by osmosis. Acting as though nothing unusual had occurred. And for him, she supposed, nothing had.

Giving herself a mental shake, Delaney took her seat. She couldn't worry about Travis Forsythe and his whims. He'd forget about her soon enough when something bright and shiny caught his eye.

But still. Travis *was* a puzzle.

THE WEEK PASSED quickly. Travis didn't have time to pursue his friendship with Delaney. She would have been surprised to find out how often she entered his thoughts. Usually when he was lifting weights or running laps.

When his body was occupied with repetitive workouts, his mind always drifted. More often than not, he ended up thinking about Delaney.

As long as Travis could remember, he thought she was strange. If he thought of her at all. Now, he realized the problem didn't lie with Delaney, but with him. With all the students at Green Hills High School. They were so wrapped up in their own lives that they couldn't be bothered to see what had always been right in front of them.

Delaney wasn't strange. She was lonely.

One look into her eyes and he knew. Perhaps the age difference was the culprit. Or the fact that she was just so much damn smarter than the rest of them. For whatever reason, she hadn't made friends after the administration skipped her ahead a few grades.

The idea that he could help curb a bit of Delaney's loneliness might seem odd. But in some ways, Travis needed a friend as much as she did.

Weighed down by expectations, he sometimes felt isolated from the people he'd known his entire life.

Travis' father wanted him to be a success. Alan Forsythe's dreams rested on his son stepping higher than he had. Pick an occupation. He didn't care. Baseball player. Mathematician. The job didn't matter. Alan didn't want Travis to live from paycheck to paycheck, always wondering if next month would bring the day he didn't have enough money in the bank to meet his obligations.

Then there were Travis' friends. His peers.

The girls wanted to hang off the arm of a famous athlete. The guys wanted to latch onto a future superstar. Even Eddie—the person Travis would have once sworn could never be blinded by celebrity—seemed more and more interested in the time when he could start sponging off his famous buddy.

Eddie always laughed off his comments. But each time— delivered with increased frequency—Travis felt a wave of unease he found harder and harder to shake off.

"There you are," Eddie called out. Dressed in street clothes, he fell in step with Travis, puffing hard before they finished a half lap of the track. "What's the deal running during lunch hour?"

Travis had a fairly steady workout routine. In fact, most days one could set one's watch by it. However, there were times when his dad needed help on a job. After school today, instead of hitting the gym, he'd be on his way to the nearby town of Prescott.

"If Dad doesn't finish Mrs. Banks' roof today, he'll miss out on the job rewiring Mayor Detwiler's hunting lodge."

"So, skip running for one day."

"Can't," Travis said, not missing a stride when Eddie stopped. "Don't want to fall behind."

Eddie bent over, resting his hands on his knees. Using the last of his breath, he yelled, "You're a freaking machine, man."

Travis chuckled, increasing his speed. Four more laps. He could have easily done ten, but time wasn't on his side. Tomorrow, he promised himself.

Out of the corner of his eye, Travis caught a streak of dark gray. Delaney rushing toward the music room. Funny. A week ago, he wouldn't have noticed how fast she was when she wanted to be. Or how she stayed as close to the buildings as possible in an attempt to blend in—to go undetected.

Those days were over.

At least as far as Travis was concerned.

IF SHE WERE asked, Delaney wouldn't have been able to explain exactly how Travis managed to finagle his way into her life.

If he'd pushed, she would have been able to push back—in her own way. Force she understood. After living in the same house as Munch Brill for seven years, Delaney was practically an expert.

Travis wasn't a bull, getting his way by smashing everything in his path. He was more subtle. Like a big, blue-eyed puppy. Seemingly harmless and impossible to resist.

Her original plan to simply avoid him had been doable; she was certain he'd grow bored with the novelty of hanging around the weird girl. Travis didn't really want a new friend. He wanted a challenge. A new, unusual way to pass his time between school and working out—he always seemed to be running in circles or lifting weights.

Or—what was the term—shagging balls? Why did so many things that had to do with sports sound slightly risqué? Even downright dirty?

Delaney smiled at her wayward musings.

"Want to share the joke?"

She glanced at Travis, swerving back to her original train of thought. He walked her home most days. Through the back alleys where nobody could see them. The first time, Delaney had insisted he stop two blocks from her house. Travis hadn't asked why, as if understanding the subject wasn't open for debate.

Maybe *that* was the secret to his method. Travis recognized Delaney's boundaries, immediately backing away when she tensed or became uncomfortable. Yet, he never gave up.

A month of walking by her side. A month of innocent conversations about school. Or his father's current job. Or how old Delaney was when she first began playing the piano.

They were on the cusp of friendship. Which was why Delaney felt comfortable enough to tease Travis for the first time.

"Why do guys who are innately homophobic have no problem playing with each other's balls?"

Travis stopped in his tracks.

"Excuse me?"

"You know. Baseballs. Basketballs. Footballs," she clarified.

When Travis' expression didn't change, Delaney wondered if she'd made an error in judgment. Had she offended him with her joke? And if so, how would he retaliate? She inched away, ready to flee. Then, to her relief, Travis threw his head back and laughed.

"You are full of surprises. Smart *and* a sense of humor." Travis wiped the moisture from his eyes.

As Delaney tipped her head up so she could look Travis directly in the face—a move she wouldn't have considered until recently—she automatically raised a hand to push her glasses up her nose. But they weren't there. The moment they were alone, Travis would take away the frames with the clear glass, keeping them in his pocket as they walked.

At first, Delaney protested. Travis simply ignored her. Now, she handed the glasses over without a second thought.

"Don't you miss riding your motorcycle to school?"

Travis shrugged.

"The damn machine is broken down more often than not. Besides, I like walking. With you. Unless I can talk you into riding with me."

The twinkle in his blue eyes told Delaney Travis wasn't serious. He was so sure she wouldn't agree to get behind him on his bike. But he was wrong. If circumstances were different—if she weren't certain Munch would blow a gasket—Delaney wouldn't hesitate.

She wanted to believe her streak for adventure—the one she'd embraced as a child—lurked deep inside. The longing to take a ride behind Travis gave her hope.

"I want to. But…"

"When you're ready, I'll take you." Travis sent her a sideways grin. "If the motor on that old machine cooperates."

"Really?" Delaney heard the neediness in her voice but didn't care.

"I promise."

"Thank you."

"I haven't done anything yet," Travis said, his smile warm.

"Yes. You have."

Before Travis could ask her what she meant, Delaney snatched her glasses from his pocket, turned, running the rest of the way home. She slowed her gait before entering the house—Munch insisted she conduct herself in a ladylike manner. Taking the stairs, she shut her door, falling onto her bed with a happy sigh.

Travis had given Delaney something to look forward to—even if she never found the chance to take him up on his offer

"Delaney?" Alma's voice echoed down the long hall. "Put your things away and come help me with dinner."

Carefully, Delaney placed her school books in a neat pile on the small desk. Neat as a pin—just like the rest of her room. Before she left, she smoothed the blanket on the twin bed, straightening her pillow.

She hated the faded pink sheets splashed with pale yellow daisies. Just as she hated the twin bed with the carved white headboard. And the pile of stuffed animals that seemed to mock her from their perch on the window seat. Even the attached bathroom was pink from the walls to towels to the toilet.

The decor was Munch's idea. His way of keeping Delaney a little girl—until...

Hastily, Delaney left the room. With a firm pull, she closed the door, wishing she could shut off her thoughts as easily. Why couldn't she have held onto the dream of riding on Travis' motorcycle just a little longer?

Because this house is filled with fear and sadness. The walls seemed to sniff out any hint of happiness with frightening efficiency. Not so long ago she would have said the same about the town in which she lived.

Abandon hope all ye who enter here. True, Dante hadn't written about Green Hills However, the sentiment fit well enough.

Lately, when Delaney walked outside, she could feel a change in the air. She had a friend. She had somebody to laugh with. Something to look forward to.

Delaney—at least for now—had Travis.

CHAPTER SIX

● ≈ ● ≈ ●

MAY WAS DELANEY'S favorite time of the year.

For one month—without fail—Munch went to Mexico. He and varying members of his family made the trip to do who knew what—Delaney didn't care. He was gone, and that was all that mattered.

"Pancakes for breakfast?" Alma asked as she passed by Delaney's bedroom, her arms filled with freshly washed laundry.

Delaney wouldn't say her mother had a bounce in her step—the weight of the world had been bearing down on her shoulders for too long. But her voice sounded lighter. As if the ever-present world had been—at least temporarily—replaced by a mere continent.

"With blueberries?"

Munch liked a healthy breakfast, and he expected his *girls* to eat the same way. Alma didn't go crazy when he was away—she never knew when one of his spies might drop by for a *friendly* visit.

However, their first morning of temporary freedom was special. They splurged on food Munch never allowed them to have.

70

Strong coffee—borrowed from their neighbor Mrs. Thomas, a woman who understood a thing or two about controlling husbands—and pancakes with lots and lots of real maple syrup—again, courtesy of their neighbor.

"Mr. Bingley at the farmer's market had the first blueberries of the season. I was able to snatch up the last two containers. Ten minutes?"

"I'll be there."

Delaney finished combing out her long hair, slightly damp from her morning shower. She didn't own a blow dryer, not that she cared. She wasn't interested in wasting time to get the heavy length completely moisture free, only to clamp it back into a severe, boringly ubiquitous, ponytail.

What she really wanted to do was hack the thing off. Short hair would be so much nicer. So much more flattering.

Delaney picked up the small silver hand mirror—the last gift her father had given her—and studied her face. She'd never be a beauty. But with a little effort, she might be pretty.

Her long, angular face could benefit from a little color. Blush on her naturally pale cheeks. Her eyelashes were bad, but some mascara would be a nice complement. And her lips—neither particularly full nor thin? Delaney longed to cover them in crimson. Or bright fire-engine red. Maybe a startling neon orange. Anything, as long as the color was bold.

One day, Delaney promised herself as she used a brown plastic clip to subdue her long, brown hair. She'd surround herself in bright hues of yellow, and blue, and red.

Silently, she chuckled. Seemed she'd made a lot of promises to herself lately. The reason was simple. Delaney was tired of living a drab, stilted, muted life. One day, she'd find the color she knew existed beyond Green Hills, South Carolina.

Taking the stairs two at a time, Delaney breathed deeply. Munch had only been gone a few hours, and already the air was sweeter. Filled with the scent of coffee, blueberry pancakes, maple syrup, and...

Pausing, Delaney breathed in again. Bacon? She smiled. Oh, yes. May was definitely the best month of the year.

"WHICH TEAM DO you think will draft you?"

"Probably Seattle. Maybe San Diego."

"Seattle sucks," Eddie said with lip curling disgust. "Not that San Diego is any great shakes. But at least the weather is better."

"The teams with the worst records get the first picks," Travis shrugged, shoving his cleats into his old, Army surplus duffle.

"Shitty system. But on the bright side, the higher you get drafted, the better the signing bonus. *Cha-ching.*"

Before he could snap at Eddie, Travis bit his tongue. Lately, all his friend could talk about was money. Baseball money. Travis' baseball money.

With a sigh, Travis ran a hand through his hair, counting to ten. Maybe he didn't see things clearly. Eddie was his friend. Naturally, he was excited about the Major League Baseball Draft. He wanted his buddy to land on a good team. If he seemed obsessed with money—money Travis had yet to earn—so what? Neither of them had grown up surrounded by wealth. A little cash in the bank was a heady idea.

Green Hills had just defeated their division rivals—twice. Doubleheaders weren't the norm, but they had to make up a rainout from earlier in the season. After eighteen innings in which Travis had contributed with some stellar defense and six hits, including a home run and a bases-clearing double, all he wanted was a good dinner, a few hours vegging in front of some mindless television, followed by an early night.

Now wasn't the best time to have Eddie and his dreams of dollar signs, buzzing around. Normally, Travis saw his friend as slightly overeager, but relatively harmless. Today, he felt more like an annoying gnat.

All Travis wanted to do was swat him away. Instead, he ignored Eddie's comments, swinging his duffle over his shoulder before heading out of the locker room.

The season was in full swing, and Green Hills looked like they could finally bring home a state championship—an achievement Travis would have missed if not for his father's insistence he finish high school.

Thank you, Dad. Travis planned on using a big chunk of his signing bonus to buy his father a much-needed new truck. The least he could do after all the years of unwavering support and sacrifice.

What was left—if anything—would be slated straight for the bank. Travis wouldn't piss away his money on frivolous purchases and partying. No matter what hopes Eddie might harbor.

"A bunch of the gang is meeting out at Tillman's Quarry. Burt *acquired*," grinning, Eddie made exaggerated air quotes, "a keg from the basement of his dad's bar. I'm catching a ride with Janey. See you there?"

Tillman's was *the* place for high school drinking and other shenanigans. More than one teenager had lost their virginity while hopped up on beer and whatever drug made party rounds. Once or twice, an unwanted pregnancy could be traced back to a wild Saturday night at the quarry.

Suddenly, Travis felt older than his years. Or maybe—with his dreams so close—he'd outgrown the need to fill the small-town boredom with booze and casual sex. Either way, the thought of joining the gang made him a little sad.

And more tired than playing two full, nine-inning baseball games.

"I think I'll skip the fun this time."

"You've skipped the fun a lot lately." Eddie crossed his arms, a frown marring his freckled brow. "Is she the reason?"

Travis glanced to where Eddie indicated with a jerk of his head, just catching sight of Delaney before the door to the music room closed behind her.

"People are starting to talk about you and Dippy Delaney."

"Stop calling her that. Or any of the other names you use. She's Delaney."

Eddie snorted.

"I'm serious, Eddie."

"Serious? About Dippy—" All Travis had to do was raise an eyebrow. Eddie recognized the look, though this was the first time the warning had been directed his way. He closed his mouth, but he wasn't happy with the turn of events.

"Do you want to know why you think Delaney is strange?" Travis asked as he stored his bag on the back of his motorcycle.

"Because she is? Sorry." Eddie raised his hands as if trying to ward off his oldest friend's displeasure.

Travis gave Eddie some slack. He couldn't condemn his friend for a crime he'd been guilty of not so long ago.

"Delaney is shy. Introverted. Instead of trying to see past her insecurities, we branded her. Strange. *Dippy*. Yes, she's different. Smarter than the rest of us. Younger. Not as experienced. But different isn't necessarily a bad thing."

Eddie shrugged, not ready to concede Travis' point.

Travis sighed, searching his brain for a way to explain that Eddie would understand. His lips twitched when an idea popped.

"Remember when we were around eight, maybe nine? The old shed by your house?"

"Maybe." Leary, Eddie's eyes narrowed.

"You wouldn't go near the thing because you were convinced a monster lived inside. All the creaks and groans when the wind blew had you freaked out."

"Freaked out is a bit of an exaggeration."

Travis snorted.

"Come on, man. I was there. You practically crapped your pants when your dad finally had enough and dragged you out there."

Eddie's father, flashlight in one hand, holding his son by the scruff of the neck with the other, examined every inch of that old shed. Under the rotting boards. The cobweb-covered corners. Twenty minutes later, no more monsters.

"The unknown is always scary. Try getting to know Delaney. She's worth the effort."

Slowly, Eddie nodded, as if giving Travis' words serious thought.

"You've forgotten the most important thing about that old shed."

"What's that?"

"The monster didn't disappear until the next day when Dad bulldozed the motherfucker. Razed the bastard to the ground." Eyes sharp as daggers, Eddie smiled slowly. "Then burned the remains to nothing but ashes."

Travis felt a sick lump form in his stomach.

"Jesus, Eddie."

"Lighten up, man. Can't you take a joke anymore?" Eyes clearing, a chuckle slipping past his lips, Eddie patted Travis on the back. "Enjoy your new little friend. If you change your mind about the party, you know where to find us. If not, see you Monday."

Watching as Eddie jumped into the cab of his girlfriend's late-model pickup, Travis wondered if the boy he thought he'd known for all these years had changed. Or had he been blind to a dark side that always lurked beneath the surface?

Since they could crawl, they had been like brothers. Mischief making. Secret sharing. Imagining their futures.

He was tired, Travis decided, blaming his restless sleep instead of Eddie.

Late at night, darkness invaded his thoughts as well as his bedroom, bringing nerves he hadn't realized he possessed and a trace of doubt to his—up until now—unflagging belief in his talent.

Maybe he wasn't good enough to play professional baseball at the highest level. Maybe he'd flame out, end up back in Green Hills, trudging through each day with nothing to look forward to but a nine-to-five, nowhere job and bitter regrets.

When the sun rose the next morning, Travis woke with renewed optimism. But the little voice of doom wasn't gone, simply waiting, making him toss and turn when normally, he'd sleep like a log. His brain clear and untroubled.

Shaking his head, Travis pocketed his keys, jogging across the lawn. Placing his hand on the door, he paused, music reaching his ears. The melody entered his blood, relaxing his tense muscles, easing his mind. Quietly, he entered the room.

Travis could have spent all day trying to explain to Eddie the connection he felt to Delaney. But why waste his time when *he* didn't understand completely? On the surface, they had little in common. But they could talk nonstop about nothing in particular. Or simply walk side by side, the silence never feeling awkward.

Friends. Pure and simple.

"I know you're there," Delaney said without breaking the flow of the song.

"Naturally. You have eyes in the back of your head." In a few long strides, Travis covered the distance between them. "Besides, I wasn't trying to hide."

Delaney raised her head, her eyes—a clear, pure purple—unobstructed by the glasses that sat on the piano. Lips curved in a small, but welcoming smile.

"Then why stand in the shadows?"

"The acoustics are better over by the door."

"Okay." Her smile widened, not buying his excuse for a second.

Travis shrugged.

"Sometimes when you know I'm watching, you stop."

"You made me nervous."

Her fingers flew over the keys, ending in a flourish Travis could appreciate but never dream of duplicating.

"I *made* you nervous? Not anymore?"

"Not anymore."

Delaney lowered her hands to her lap. Once, she would have clasped her fingers together, her knuckles white. She would have kept her head down, her eyes averted.

Gaze steady, chin held high, hands relaxed, the way Delaney held her body told a tale beyond her words.

No. Travis didn't make her nervous. Not anymore.

"I didn't expect you to come to the game."

"How did you...?" Delaney frowned. "I didn't think anybody noticed me."

"You can't hide from me." Travis grinned. "Not anymore."

"I should embroider that on a pillow."

"You embroider?"

"Badly," she admitted. "But if pressed, I could do a few simple words."

"If pressed, I'll buy us t-shirts."

Laughing, Delaney reached for her glasses. Travis was faster.

"What would happen if I accidentally stepped on these things?" Casually, he tossed the frames in the air, catching them easily. "Again and again?"

The look in Delaney's eyes told him she wouldn't mind if his questions become a reality. Still, she held her hand out, waiting until Travis gave her back the glasses.

"My stepfather would buy me another pair. As soon as he gets back from Mexico."

Travis didn't know Munch Brill beyond recognizing him on the street. But if he were anything like the rest of his family, living with the man couldn't have been easy.

The Brills weren't particularly liked around Green Hills.

"When did your stepfather leave?"

"Yesterday."

"How long will he be gone?"

If a sigh could tell a story, Delaney's did. Happiness and joy. They looked good on her.

"A month. Four whole weeks."

"Thirty-one days?" Travis grinned, her mood contagious.

"If we're lucky."

"Delaney—"

Travis didn't know what questions to ask. He wanted to help. But how?

Before he could think of something—anything—Delaney tossed her own question his way. And surprised all other thoughts from his head.

"Can we go for a ride on your motorcycle?"

"Now?"

The hope that briefly sparkled in her eyes died a quick death.

"I suppose you have plans." Delaney's chin dropped to her chest with a dejected sigh. "Saturday night at Tillman's Quarry."

"What do you know about the quarry?"

"Everybody knows, even if they aren't invited."

Travis couldn't picture Delaney standing around an impromptu bonfire, a beer in her hand.

"You want to go?"

"Not really. But I wouldn't mind if someone had asked—at least once."

"Now I feel guilty."

"Good." Delaney squared her shoulders. "I'm not the only one who's been left out, Travis. Look around sometime. You might be surprised how many kids go unnoticed. People you might like if you gave them a chance."

Hadn't he said almost the same thing to Eddie not thirty minutes earlier? Talk about his words coming back to bite him.

"Well, shit."

"Exactly," Delaney nodded. "Don't beat yourself up, Travis. You did a good deed by me. One charity case is enough for anybody."

"You're my friend, Delaney." Travis took her hand—one of the few times he'd touched her. But he wanted her to understand. "Friends. From the beginning."

Delaney looked at their joined hands, then looked at Travis. Her eyes—God, those eyes—were like a punch to his gut and ray of sunlight all tangled up together.

"I know."

"Good. Still want to go for that ride?"

"Really?"

Travis laughed. For the first time that he could remember, Delaney's face lit with excitement. She looked like what she was. A fifteen-year-old girl.

"But you can't go wearing that."

A little of the light left her eyes as she touched her baggy dress.

"I don't have anything else."

"Don't worry. I do."

CHAPTER SEVEN

● ≈ ● ≈ ●

TRAVIS RACED THE bike up the mountain road, controlling the powerful machine with practiced ease. Behind him, Delaney held on tight, her laughter about the sweetest sound he'd ever heard.

Slowing down, he turned off the pavement onto dirt and gravel. The back wheel fishtailed, but Travis regained control quickly.

"Don't worry," Travis yelled over his shoulder when Delaney squeezed him harder. "I won't let anything happen to you."

"I know."

A simple response, but filled with absolute conviction. Only human—a teenager through and through—Travis felt a flash of pride. Followed by a warm glow that spread over his body.

Delaney trusted him.

Not completely. Not with her deepest secrets. However, the fact that she was sitting behind him was a huge step. A few months ago, she never would have agreed, let alone made the suggestion. Progress, indeed.

Travis couldn't pinpoint the exact moment when the thick walls she'd built around herself had lowered enough to let him in.

Slowly. Steadily. Their casual conversations had taken on a deeper meaning.

If not with words, then the way she could look him in the eyes without hesitation. Or the smile on her lips when she didn't know he watched.

And, Travis could say without hesitation—the feeling of ease went both ways.

Another turn, then one more, Travis brought the bike to a stop.

"What a beautiful spot. How did you know it was here?"

"A few years ago, Dad and I were up here doing a job. On the way home, we had a flat. Changing a tire is pretty much a one-man job. So, to pass the time, I took a walk. My wandering brought me here."

In the center of the small, secluded area was a grass-covered hill perfect for a person to sit and think. Or take a nap. Or simply stare at the sky. Since that day, Travis had come back to do all three—depending on his mood.

However, he'd always come alone. Until Delaney.

"I feel like we're surrounded by an oasis. Without the sand. Or palm trees."

Chuckling, Travis swung his leg over the bike, removing his helmet. Delaney's observations weren't so far off from his thoughts the first time he walked into the clearing.

"No camels either. Sorry."

"Too bad. If there were camels, we wouldn't be in South Carolina."

Travis couldn't miss the touch of wistful longing that filled Delaney's voice.

"You want to be someplace else?"

"I want a lot of things." Delaney removed her helmet, setting it on the seat of the bike. "And one day, I'll get them."

No longer wistful, Delaney sounded determined, a touch of unexpected steel entering her tone. Travis understood need. Want and desperation were his old friends. The feelings burned in his gut 24/7.

Delaney knew Travis' plans. Hell, the entire town of Green Hills knew. But she hadn't shared what she wanted after they graduated. And because she always tensed up when their conversations turned too personal, he hadn't asked.

Travis was tired of pussyfooting around. They were friends. Delaney trusted him not to smash her body into a million pieces. Why shouldn't she trust him with her dreams?

"What do you want to do with your life, Del?"

As she turned her head, her eyes met his. Purple. Dark. Intense.

"I want to live."

For a moment, Travis didn't think Delaney meant to elaborate. She slowly walked around the clearing, her fingers lightly dancing over a patch of wildflowers.

Delaney looked a fraction of her age, like a little girl in the middle of playing dress-up. The leather jacket he'd loaned her was three sizes too big, hanging loose on her slight frame. And though the hem of the blue jeans hit her several inches above her ankles, the waist gaped a bit, her slim hips not close to filling out the denim in the same way as the original owner.

However, when she reached up, loosening her hair until the long, dark locks fell free down her back, Travis caught a glimpse of who she'd be a few years down the road.

Her face bathed in the late afternoon sun, he knew that with a little seasoning—a touch of experience to add interest to her still maturing countenance—Delaney would turn heads in every room she entered.

Striking more than beautiful. Something about her would demand a second look. Then a third.

Like him—at this moment—nobody would be able to take their eyes off her.

"I want to wake up every morning free to make my own decisions. Free to wear what I want. Eat what I want. Talk to whomever I want." Delaney sighed. "I want…"

"Freedom?" Travis teased. Didn't all kids want to do whatever they wanted?

Instead of the answering smile he expected, Delaney's expression turned grave—deadly serious.

"Yes."

Then, before Travis could respond, her face cleared, light replacing dark.

"The clothes?" Delaney slipped off the jacket, swinging it back and forth on her outstretched hand. "Where did you get them?"

"They were in the saddle bags on my bike."

"Ah," Delaney said as if she suddenly understood everything.

Normally, Travis enjoyed when a twinkle entered Delaney's gaze. But not this time.

"Whatever you think you know, you're wrong." He found himself on the defensive, and not happy to be there. "You aren't the first girl to ride behind me on my bike."

Delaney's lips twitched, obviously enjoying Travis' discomfort.

"You sent her home naked?"

"No." Travis snatched the jacket from Delaney. "She'd consumed a little too much beer." A lot of beer, if Travis' memory served him right. "We—and some friends—went swimming. She had her bathing suit on under her clothes. We argued. She chose to ride home with somebody else."

"Without her clothes?"

"You're awfully inquisitive today." Unusual for Delaney. A sudden thought hit Travis, one that put a smile back on his lips. "If I tell you the whole story, will you answer a few questions of mine?"

"Sure."

"Really?"

"However, I reserve the right not to answer."

He should have known there would be a catch. Perhaps Delaney dreamed of becoming a lawyer. The way her mind worked certainly seemed suited to the profession.

"Tell you what." Travis took his usual seat. On the hill. In the shade of an old oak tree. He patted the ground, an invitation for Delaney to join him. "I'll finish my story about the jacket and jeans. Then you can tell me about your plans after we graduate next month."

Delaney sank to the ground, her legs crossed. She wore a t-shirt—a spare Travis always carried with him. Baggy as her everyday dresses, at least she'd knotted the ends at her waist.

"What my plans are? Nothing else?"

"I have a million questions." Travis relaxed on the ground, his hands behind his head. "We'll start with that one."

Delaney copied him, so they were lying side by side.

"Okay. You first."

"The first week in April a few of us went out to Dawson's Pond. The weather had turned warm, around eighty degrees."

"I remember."

"I gave Meg Drake a ride."

"Is she your girlfriend?"

"She's a girl who's a friend."

"Semantics."

"Fact," Travis corrected.

When Delaney laughed, Travis closed his eyes and recounted the story of what started out as a casual get-together. After too much beer, Meg decided to jump in the pond even though everybody else decided the water was too cold.

"She managed to take off her clothes. But the second she hit the water, the beer hit her—hard. She tried to kiss me. I held her off. There were tears. And a lot of screaming about God only knows what. Meg ended up going home with Stacy Prescott, I ended up with Meg's clothes."

"And you still have them."

"Mm." Travis ran a hand over his face. "Kind of a complicated situation."

"You take the clothes and hand them back. What's complicated about that?"

"How much experience do you have dealing with emotional teenage girls?"

The second the words were out of his mouth, Travis wished them back. Delaney was a loner—whatever the reasons. Through sheer stubbornness, he'd pulled her partially out of the shadows. He looked forward to the time they spent together.

Snarky comments about her lack of friends was a great way to ruin the progress they had made.

To Travis' surprise, Delaney didn't take offense.

"I may not be friends with any teenage girls. But I *am* one."

"You aren't like other girls."

"Thanks a lot," Delaney said with a rueful chuckle.

"Believe me, I just paid you a huge compliment." Rolling to his side, Travis propped his head on his hand, his gaze on Delaney's relaxed face. "I can talk to you without worrying about the usual crap."

"You mean you aren't attracted to me?"

"No. Not that you aren't pretty," he hastened to assure her.

"Relax, Travis." Delaney turned. Calm and clear, her eyes met his. "We work as friends because neither of us wants anything more."

Travis relaxed. He would have bet almost anything that he and Delaney were on the same page. To hear her confirm his belief was a huge relief.

"Meg wouldn't take back her clothes," he continued with his story. "I planned on leaving her stuff in her locker, but time passed, and I never got around to it.

"Why wouldn't she take her clothes?"

"I don't know."

"Sure you do," Delaney said. "As long as you have her jacket and jeans, she thinks she has a hold on you. Superficial or not. Throw them in the trash—after I'm done with them. End of story."

"Shouldn't I give Meg another chance? The jacket is leather."

"Nope. Make a clean break. If you don't, Meg will continue to think she has a chance. Unless you want her?"

"I don't want anybody. Not now. Not until I know my career has taken off."

"There you go."

"How come you're so smart about this boy/girl stuff?"

"I read. A lot."

Travis nodded. "Psychology books?"

"Some. But you would be amazed what goes on in YA romance novels."

"You're kidding."

"Don't look so surprised. There are some really good writers out there. Mostly they teach me what not to do. And how not to act."

"You give good advice

The light in Delaney's eyes dimmed.

"Advice is easy when somebody else's problems are involved."

"I might not have the answers you need, but I can listen."

Slowly, Delaney shook her head. Her lips curved upward, but the smile didn't reach her eyes.

"Thank you, Travis. But no."

Travis would have argued if he thought his words would do any good. Since he knew better, he dropped the subject. For now.

"I shared my tale. Your turn. What are your post-graduation plans?"

"Promise not to tell anyone?"

Intrigued, Travis perked up.

"Secrets? Count me in."

Delaney raised a brow and waited.

"I promise, Del. My lips are sealed." Travis made his point by locking his lips with a turn of his wrist and throwing away the imaginary key.

"I was accepted at the University of Hawaii. The offered me a full-ride scholarship."

"Congratulations." Confused, Travis frowned. "Why is your choice of school a secret?"

"My stepfather wants me to attend someplace closer."

A full-ride and Hawaii? Delaney's smarts had truly paid off. Big time.

"Screw someplace closer. Your stepfather is crazy."

"Yes," Delaney nodded, looking into space. "Crazy about sums him up."

"Del…"

She jumped to her feet. "I better get going. Mom expects me for dinner, and she tends to worry."

"Sure."

Travis walked to where he parked his bike, handing Delaney her helmet and borrowed jacket. Taking his seat, he turned the ignition. The motor coughed but started without too much fuss. He waited for Delaney to join him. When her arms were around his waist, he raised the kickstand.

"Delaney," he said, worried by the direction their conversation had taken. "You won't let anything—anybody—stop you from going to Hawaii. Will you?"

Though Delaney's voice was low and the engine loud, Travis had no problem hearing her. Or the steely determination that punctuated each word as she tightened her grip.

"Munch is used to getting his way. But not this time."

"WHERE HAVE YOU been?"

Delaney had expected her mother to meet her at the door. Dressed in her own clothes, her hair in a neat ponytail. No clues remained to the hours she'd spent with Travis.

"At school. You know how I get when I play. All sense of time shoots out the window."

The lie fell easily from her lips. Her mother might think she wanted the truth. However, for both their sakes, the less Alma knew, the better.

"He has people watching, Laney."

Whispered, as if the walls of the house had ears, Alma's words sent a frigid shiver down Delaney's spine. She knew that Munch had spies. Green Hills was thick with his family members. Not to mention the innumerable people in debt to the Brills. Or who took a few bucks every week under the table. Their job? Keep a close eye on their neighbor's comings and goings.

Delaney and Alma weren't the only people who interested the Brill family. They kept a close watch on the town. Adultery. Theft. The more unsavory the offense, the better.

The mayor used the information to solidify his hold on the office. The sheriff did the same. Munch didn't worry about leaving town. If Alma or Delaney made a false step, he'd find out soon enough.

Heat replaced the cold down Delaney's spine, suffusing her blood. She was so tired of living in fear. Tired. Period.

"Let's leave."

"What?" Alma gasped, clutching the dishtowel that seemed permanently glued to her hand.

"Grab a bag. We'll ask Mrs. Thomas to drive us to the Greyhound station in Billings. From there, we can go anywhere we want."

"We can't."

Alma rushed down the hall toward her only refuge—the kitchen. Delaney was right behind her.

"We can. I have some money."

For years, Delaney had saved every penny she could get her hands on. Munch wasn't very good at keeping track of how much cash he had in his wallet at any given time. And Delaney didn't feel an ounce of remorse stealing a dollar—or five—any chance she had.

Under the loose board in her closet sat a roll of bills. Almost six hundred in cash. Not a fortune. But enough to give them a good head start.

"No. He'll find us. He always knows, Laney. Always."

Alma checked the casserole in the oven, her hands visibly shaking. Worried she might burn herself, Delaney removed their dinner before leading her mother to the table. Gently—but firmly—she sat her down.

"I'm not a little girl like the last time, Mom. If Munch comes after us, we can fight back. Scream, if nothing else. He can't *make* us come back."

"Yes, he can. He'll have me locked away."

"Away? Where?"

"State mental hospital."

"Mom—"

"I've seen the papers, Laney." Alma clutched at Delaney, her eyes wild with fear. "They're already signed by Munch and his uncle in the next county. All Judge Brill has to do is date and file them."

Delaney could feel the fear radiating from her mother. And she didn't blame her. Munch wasn't above committing his wife.

"As soon as we cross the South Carolina state line, we'll go to a women's shelter." Delaney had done her research. "They won't send you back to an abusive husband. And they have lawyers who will help."

Furiously shaking her head, Alma wheezed, unable to fully catch her breath.

"No place is safe. No place is safe."

Tears ran down Alma's face. Delaney fell to her knees, drawing her mother close.

"Shh," she crooned. "Everything will be all right."

"We'll stay? Promise?"

"Everything will be all right."

As she wiped her mother's cheeks, Delaney accepted what deep down she'd always known. Alma was too afraid to run. Too beaten down. Her prison had become her home, and she couldn't imagine life outside the bar-free doors.

Delaney swallowed, fighting back a few tears of her own. When she left Green Hills—and she was more determined than ever to get away—she'd leave alone.

CHAPTER EIGHT

● ≈ ● ≈ ●

THE OLD DOOR squeaked a familiar greeting as Travis entered the house. An oddity considering the place belonged to a handyman and his handy son.

They quickly took care of all the big jobs, but little things, like oiling a noisy hinge, often fell by the wayside, unattended, since the lady of the house—the heart of their home—was no longer around to supply not-so-subtle reminders.

Travis made a mental note to tell Delaney about the squeak, imagining her gentle laugh. Then, he had to chuckle at himself.

He didn't know exactly when the girl had latched herself so firmly into his thoughts. But she had. And he wasn't the least bit upset by the revelation. In fact, Delaney had enjoyed their ride so much—and having her along had given him so much pleasure—he couldn't wait for the next time.

Soon, Travis had promised her when he dropped Delaney off a few blocks from her house. The smile she'd bestowed on him was a gift he'd treasure for a long time.

"Dad? Are you home?" Travis called out, heading to the kitchen for a glass of juice.

"I'm up here."

"Are you in the bathroom?" Travis asked, a little disappointed. He'd planned on taking a shower. They had two bathrooms, but the other one only sported a claw-foot tub. Since he wasn't fond of what he considered an exercise in sitting in a pool of his own filth, he could wait.

"I'm in bed."

Travis frowned. His father sounded exhausted. Not an uncommon occurrence on a week of long hours that started just after dawn and often didn't end before dark.

But the fact that Alan's old pickup wasn't parked in its usual place in the driveway had given Travis pause. Now, instead of relaxing in front of the television with a beer and a bowl of chips—as was his habit on Saturday—his father was already down for the night?

"What's up?" Travis asked, standing in the bedroom door.

Alan, propped up on a stack of pillows, shifted. He let out a long breath—more a grimace than a sigh.

"Hurt my back."

His father clenched his teeth as if trying to hold the pain in check. Injuries came with Alan's profession. However, Travis had never known anything to lay the man low. If his father had given in enough to admit something was wrong, the problem had to be bad.

"Did you stop to see Dr. Crenshaw?"

"That old quack?" Just shaking his head made the lines deepen on Alan's face. "What could he do except tell me to do exactly what I did. Go home, crawl into bed, and rest."

True, Travis conceded silently. Crenshaw had been the town doctor since the crack of time. He wasn't a great healer, but he did have a supply of the good stuff.

"A couple painkillers would help you sleep," Travis called out as he crossed the hall.

"Pills aren't the answer," Alan groaned. "Advice to live by when you're out on your own surrounded by teammates with easy access to drugs. Taking something for every ache and pain is a slippery slope to drug addiction. They test for that stuff now—even in the minor leagues."

In the bathroom, Travis grabbed the bottle of *Advil*, shaking out three tablets. Though his father's warning wasn't new, the words registered. Like Alan, he believed in *playing through the pain*. Times like these, there had to be an exception.

"Here." Travis held out the pills. He set a glass of water on the nightstand.

He expected some resistance. When Alan didn't argue, swallowing the tablets without hesitation, Travis felt another surge of concern.

"What happened, Dad?"

"That freaking hunting lodge. I've been working my ass off on Detwiler's hellhole for almost a month—without much progress."

Mayor Horace Detwiler. Munch Brill's uncle. Brill, Delaney's stepfather. Sometimes he wondered how Green Hills survived. The connections were endless—and not in a good way.

Fine on the surface. The typical small town. A bit quaint. Even picturesque. However, dig a bit deeper and what would you find? A huge, incestuous pool of slimy muck.

More than ever, Travis couldn't wait to leave.

"What about the extra help Detwiler promised to hire?"

"You mean Tweedledum and Tweedledumber? Or as they like to call themselves, Mayor Detwiler's nephews?" Alan scoffed. "Hand to God, the idiot twins—as I think of them—constantly refer to themselves that way. They are more trouble than help, always arguing and getting in the way."

"Cletus and Myron Brill?"

"You know them?"

Travis pulled up a chair, stained antique white. The one his mother always sat in while she fixed her hair each morning.

"They were a few years ahead of me in school. Dumb as a sack of rocks."

Alan frowned.

"Aren't they around twenty-five?"

"Cletus and Myron were held back. More than once. I don't think they were ever going to graduate on their own. So, the school—with a little pressure from their dad—pushed them through."

"Makes sense." Alan downed the entire glass of water. "Their father is Sheriff Brill. That family takes care of their own. At the detriment of everybody else. They're the reason I hurt my back."

"Tell me what they did."

Alan explained that Cletus and Myron arrived late.

"Their bumbling has been worse than usual. Pissed off because they weren't invited on the family's yearly Mexico trip."

Travis remembered how happy Delaney seemed when she mentioned Munch was out of the country.

"I asked them to rip up some old carpet—soaked from the leaky roof."

"A leaky roof?" Travis didn't like the sound of that. "With all the rain we've had this spring? Water and electricity aren't a good mix."

"I make sure the breaker is off—and I avoid the puddles of standing water."

Travis held his tongue—barely. His father was a stickler for safety. However, the pain etched on Alan's face proved he couldn't trust Mayor Detwiler or the rest of that family to watch out for anybody but themselves.

"Cletus and Myron are always fighting. *Always*. They're big men. More fat than muscle. When they get to pushing back and forth, watch out. Before they had ripped up a single inch of carpet, Cletus took exception to something about Myron."

"His face?" Travis quipped.

Alan chuckled, which led to another pain-laced groan.

"My point, funny man, is that Myron shoved his brother. Cletus toppled over like a three-hundred-pound bowling pin. Unfortunately, he toppled onto me."

Wincing, Travis could see the picture his father painted with gut-wrenching clarity. All things considered, Alan was lucky. Cletus—and his girth—could have equaled a broken bone or two.

"Where's your truck?"

"Still at the job site. Myron and Cletus insisted on driving me home. If they don't pick me up on Monday, I'll bum a ride off somebody."

"Don't worry about your truck," Travis assured him. "Eddie and I will get it home."

"Thanks, son."

"Carpet and floors weren't part of the original deal," Travis pointed out. "Please tell me Detwiler agreed to pay you extra."

"We're in the negotiation stage."

"Fuck that, Dad." Travis gripped the edge of the bed. His father was a good man, but he wasn't always good at standing up for what was his due.

"Walk away. There's always another job."

"Not if I get on the mayor's bad side. He has the power to shut me down. Permanently."

"Then leave Green Hills. I'll be gone in a few weeks. Without Mom, what reason do you have to stay?"

"I was born and raised here, Travis. I like to think I'm fundamentally a good man."

"The best."

Pride flashed across Alan's face.

"You could be just a bit biased. But my point is simple. Green Hills won't get better if good men leave."

"What can you do against Detwiler and the Brills?"

Alan shrugged. "Maybe nothing. The only way to find out is if I stay."

The guilt Travis felt wasn't new. However, he knew with all his heart, even without baseball, his destiny wasn't in his hometown.

"I have to go."

"Damn straight." Alan gripped Travis' forearm with a warm, understanding smile. "My son is destined to be a superstar shortstop."

Travis grinned. "What happened to the man who said I can't count on making a success? Too many variables. Too many what ifs. Now you have me slated to be a superstar?"

"I wanted you to finish high school. And keep you grounded. Lucky for me, you're a pretty level-headed kid. You've made my job easy. Enough of the mush," Alan said, clearing the emotion from his throat. "I could eat something. How about you? Feel like making a couple of sandwiches."

"Ham and cheddar?"

"Sounds good." With a sigh, Alan closed his eyes. "My life would be a lot simpler if Detwiler had taken Cletus and Myron to Mexico."

The mention of Mexico made Travis think of Delaney and how happy she seemed that her stepfather was out of the country. His father had opened the door for him to ask a few questions and get the answers he couldn't get from Delaney.

"You and Munch Brill are around the same age, aren't you?"

"Mm." Between the Advil and his own bed, Alan was as close to comfortable as he'd get. "School bully. Always dated the youngest, least experienced girls he could find. Not that they stayed that way for long. He's a mean, good-for-nothing S.O.B. Still is from what I understand." Alan's eyes popped open as if his built-in dad alert system sensed trouble. "Why do you ask?"

Casually as possible, Travis shrugged.

"His stepdaughter is in my class."

"She is?" Alan frowned. "I vaguely recall Munch's wife had a kid when they married. I can't picture the girl."

"She's kind of quiet." Talk about an understatement.

"Please tell me you aren't dating Munch Brill's stepdaughter?"

"Her name is Delaney. And no. I'm not interested in dating her."

"Ah, crap." Tension re-entered Alan's expression. "You had sex with her, didn't you?"

"No!" Vehemently, Travis shook his head. "Sex with Del would be... wrong. Like getting naked with a good friend."

Travis almost said he thought of Delaney as his sister. However, he stopped himself because he didn't. For whatever reason, the distinction seemed important.

"Good. Keep that image in your head. You've managed to go this long without getting mixed up with that family. The finish line is in sight, Travis. Don't mess up now."

As Travis fixed dinner, he thought long and hard about his father's warning. If Delaney were just a girl he liked romantically, he wouldn't give her a second thought. But they were something more. Something deeper and harder to ignore.

They were friends.

If Munch Brill—or any member of his never-ending family— had a problem with Travis? Too. Damn. Bad.

CHAPTER NINE

● ≈ ● ≈ ●

FOR THE FIRST time in months, Delaney found she couldn't relax around Travis. He seemed to have the same problem. Though their reasons were as different as night and day.

Delaney needed a favor. Two, actually. But one was so big, she didn't know if she'd be able to ask the question without her stomach giving up its roiling contents. Travis might not be open to granting her wish with her vomit all over his shoes.

Over and over she'd rehearsed in her head the perfect phrasing. Every time—in the privacy of her room and the security of her thoughts—Travis said yes. Now that the time had come, she wondered which would be worse. A flat-out no. Or—Delaney swallowed—if he laughed in her face because he found the idea ridiculous.

She pulled her knees up to her chest, giving her chin someplace to rest as she waited for Travis to expel his pent-up energy.

One second he paced the length of the clearing, the next he'd flop down next to her under their usual tree. At the moment, his long legs carried him in a circle around the small piece of real estate.

"I wish you could come to the tournament," Travis said, absently tossing a baseball in the air.

The state baseball tournament would take place next week over two hundred miles away from Green Hills. Delaney didn't give a fig about sports. However, she'd enjoyed watching Travis when the team played at home. Even as a novice to the game, she recognized that he was good. Maybe great.

Travis played baseball with a joyful abandon she both admired and envied. The only thing close in her life was the piano. But music—at least for her—was a solitary exercise. She loved that she could disappear into herself for an hour or two, able to forget her troubles.

Though Delaney had no desire to take up a sport, she wondered what the camaraderie felt like. The bond created by teammates moving together toward the same goal.

Must be nice.

"I wish I could be there when you win the championship."

Travis stopped in mid-stride, turning his head in her direction. The smile she'd grown accustomed to—his lips curving slowly, showing off his straight, white teeth to perfection—lit up his face.

"We haven't won anything," Travis told her. Then, with one word, his smile turning cocky, he blew every trace of humility right out of the water. "Yet."

"Mm."

"Hey," Travis joined her on the dark-blue blanket—Delaney's contribution to their outings. "You were supposed to laugh. Or knock me down a peg or two. Why the frown, Del?"

"Munch will be back next week."

"Does he hit you?"

Eyes wide, Delaney wondered where that question had come from. The truth was just as dark. Maybe darker. Up until now, she'd never volunteered information about what Munch had planned for her. And Travis had never asked.

"Munch has never raised a hand—or his voice—to me."

"The fact that you don't like him is obvious." The blue of Travis' eyes turned a shade deeper, as did the tone of his voice. "Dad says Munch is a bully. Mean to the bone."

"Your dad is right." Delaney took a deep breath, sharing part of her secret for the first time. "Munch has never hurt me. Mom hasn't been as lucky."

"Del."

Travis moved closer, his arm tentatively going around her shoulders. A hug. Delaney couldn't remember the last time somebody touched her with no motives beyond simple comfort.

With a sigh, she settled her head on Travis' chest, soothed by the soft cotton of his t-shirt and the steady beat of his heart.

"Thank you for not asking why she doesn't leave."

"The question did occur to me."

"Me, too."

Since she was already there, Delaney twined her arms around Travis' waist. When his embrace tightened, she jumped all the way, snuggling as close as possible.

"I've finally come to terms with a bitter realization. Munch has beaten my mother so far down—physically and mentally—that she's paralyzed. She acts as if she can't remember what life was like before she married him." Delaney's fists clenched. "But I do."

"There must be someone outside of this godforsaken town who can help. Maybe if I—"

"No." Delaney shook her head, pulling back far enough to look Travis in the eyes. "You can't get involved, Travis. Munch—his family—there's no telling what they might do if you tried."

"Then what?" Delaney could feel the frustration vibrate through his body. "Something. Anything. Give me something to do."

Here was the opening Delaney needed. All she had to do was jump through. If she had the nerve.

"Do you believe a girl—" Delaney checked herself when she heard the word. From now on, she had to start thinking of herself differently. "Do you believe a young woman has the right to choose who will be her first lover?"

Travis seemed thrown by the question, as if he couldn't quite wrap his head around the concept.

"I believe," he began hesitantly, gaining conviction as he went, "everybody—woman or man—should have the right to choose their lovers. All the time. Every day. Old, young. And every age in between."

Delaney sighed, letting out a long breath. She hadn't expected Travis to answer any other way. However, he expressed her feeling so perfectly, she almost kissed him.

"Why did you ask?"

"My birthday is in June." Unable to meet Travis' narrowed gaze, Delaney focused on a spot just over his shoulder. "Some people think sixteen is just the right age."

"Some people? As in—? Holy shit." Travis gripped her arms, the bite of his fingers deep. "Your stepfather?"

Delaney gave Travis a small, almost imperceptible nod. Enough to answer his question and set him off like a heat-seeking missile. Thank goodness, his target was far away in Mexico.

"That sick, twisted son of a bitch. Has he—?"

"No."

Delaney hadn't known what she expected from Travis. Sympathy. Outrage. However, volatile didn't begin to describe the blue fire burning in his eyes.

"You have to get out of there. Today. We'll—"

"I have a plan, Travis."

"What about your mom? Scratch that," Travis waved away the thought. "From what you told me, she can barely breathe without asking permission. You can stay with Dad and me. If Munch tries to—"

"Travis. Travis!" Delaney had to stop him before he did something stupid. If he destroyed his hand—and possibly his baseball career—on the nearest tree, she'd never be able to live with herself.

"What?" Travis rounded on her, his chest rising and falling as he sucked in one outraged breath after another.

"Sit." Delaney patted the blanket. "Please."

"You're awfully calm, all things considered."

"I've had a lot longer to think things through," she said when he was beside her. Sitting, but not the least bit relaxed. "Munch will wait until my birthday. I don't know why. Sweet sixteen," Delaney shuddered. "And never been kissed. I never want to hear that phrase again as long as I live."

"Let's make sure you never have to."

Delaney swore her heart skipped a beat when Travis cupped her face, his gaze locked on her lips.

"Are we going to have sex?" she asked as he brushed his mouth across hers.

"Why don't we start with a kiss? Then we'll talk."

With a nod, Delaney waited. She'd been so worried for so long about avoiding Munch's kiss—and everything that came with it—that she hadn't given any thought to kissing a boy. Travis gave her enough time to prepare, but not enough to worry that she had no idea what she was supposed to do.

Thankfully, he'd kissed a girl or two in his time. All he required of Delaney was for her to relax—easier said than done—and decide if she liked the experience.

Sweet, was Delaney's first thought. She'd overheard some girls talking about how their dates slobbered all over them. Apparently, they had never kissed Travis. His lips were neither too wet nor too dry. Too hard or too soft. Like Goldilocks, she'd found a boy who was just right.

"What do you think?" Travis whispered as his thumb lightly caressed her cheek.

"You know what you're doing."

"I've kissed a girl. Or two," he chuckled.

"Or twenty or thirty."

"Not quite that many."

Delaney didn't care about the number. Travis didn't make her feel like one of the crowd. She felt special. At this moment, they could've been the only two people in the world.

"I was going to ask if you would have sex with me." Rather than awkward—as she expected—a sense of calm had settled over her.

"I figured." Ever so gently, Travis tucked a stray hair behind Delaney's ear.

"I even stole a condom from Marnie Tillman."

Thursday afternoon, when Delaney washed her hands in the high school bathroom, Marnie's purse sat open on the counter as she gossiped with a group of friends. The sight of an open box of condoms gave Delaney a spark of inspiration. If she lost her virginity, Munch might lose interest.

"You're the only person I would ask. The only person I can trust. But because you aren't attracted to me, I was afraid you might not be able to… You know. Perform."

When Delaney's gaze dropped to the front of Travis' jeans, a burst of color suffused her cheeks.

"I'm eighteen, Del. And a guy. A strategic gust of wind can get me hard."

"Gee, thanks."

Delaney hadn't expected Travis to gush over his newfound desire for her. But finding herself compared to a random act of nature was a little rough on her already shaky ego.

"You're very pretty, Del. And I liked kissing you," Travis reassured her. "If you want me to be your first, I'd be honored."

Unlike the rest of her life where she had no control, Travis left this choice up to her. She didn't need long to decide.

"I don't want to have sex. Not now. Not in the foreseeable future."

"Then you'll wait until you're ready." Travis took her hand. "About your stepfather?"

"I told you I have a plan. This." Delaney motioned between them "Sex with you would have been a last resort."

"Gee, thanks." With a rueful twinkle in his eyes, Travis echoed her earlier response.

"You know what I meant."

"Mm." Travis lay on his back, tugging Delaney down beside him. "Now that we've settled the will we, or won't we situation, tell me your plan."

"I won't be at our graduation."

"Where will you be?"

"On a plane headed to Hawaii."

"If you need money, I can scrape a couple hundred together."

Just like that. No questions asked. Delaney couldn't think of a single thing she'd done to deserve a friend like Travis.

"Thanks, but I have enough. I already have my ticket—and a place to stay. Ms. Watts helped me arrange everything. She was sympathetic when I said I wanted to get acclimated before classes start next fall."

"Who's Ms. Watts?"

"The guidance counselor. You never met her?"

Travis shrugged. "I've never needed any guidance."

"Depends on who you ask."

"Ha, ha." Travis shifted his gaze from the sky toward Delaney. "I agree that your plan is good—in theory."

Delaney knew where Travis was headed.

"Scum like Munch? He might decide he's waited long enough."

How many times did Delaney lie in bed, diligently going over every contingency? She couldn't plug every hole because—though she often had her doubts—Munch was human. And humans were unpredictable.

"I won't let him…" Delaney choked on the words. "I won't let him. Period. I have a knife hidden under my mattress. If all else fails, I'll—"

"No!"

"Yes! I'll kill him, Travis. If you think I'm not capable, you're wrong."

"Kill the bastard—with my blessing." Travis expelled a shaky burst of air. "I thought—"

"What?"

"I was afraid you planned on killing yourself."

"Death before dishonor?" And let Munch win? "No. Not me."

"I think I love you, Delaney Pope."

"Like a sister?"

"I wouldn't kiss my sister. Or consider having sex with her. I love you like a friend."

With Travis by her side and her secrets finally out in the open, Delaney was as close to feeling at peace as she'd get until she was far, far away from Green Hills.

She would miss him. But they had here. And now.

"I love you, too. Friend."

Delaney liked the way the words sounded. She would miss Travis. So very much. But they had here. They had now. Tomorrow was too much to ask. Somewhere. Sometime. Someday. A little part of her could always hope.

Energized, Delaney jumped to her feet. She grabbed her bag, glancing at Travis as she opened the zipper.

"Would you do me a favor?"

"Seems like an unnecessary question at this point."

"You might not think so when you hear what I want. It's pretty big."

"Bigger than divesting you of your virginity?"

Understandably cautious, Travis sat up, watching as Delaney returned, carrying a sharp, metal object.

"Hold out your hand."

"Scissors?" Travis hefted the weight. "Big-ass scissors. Do I really want to know?"

"If you're careful, no blood will be shed."

Filling her lungs with air—and courage—Delaney sat, her legs crossed, her back to Travis. Reaching up, she removed the band from her hair.

"Cut it off."

"Del." She could hear when Travis gulped. "Are you sure?"

Her first open act of defiance. What could Munch do after the fact? Yell? Make her wear a wig? If Delaney thought too hard about the possibilities, she might chicken out.

"I'm sure. Cut if off."

"I've never cut anybody's hair before."

"Just make sure you leave me both my ears and we'll be fine."

Snip. A long piece of what Delaney had come to think of as chains that wore her down hit the ground. Followed by another, then another in quick succession.

As Travis found his rhythm, divesting Delaney of her burden, her head wasn't the only part of her that felt lighter. She closed her eyes and felt her spirit soar.

"Are you going to tell me when?"

"Nope," Delaney laughed. Go as short as you can go."

"IF YOU WON'T come home with me, at least let me put a lock on your bedroom door."

Parked in the shadows of the alley, Delaney hopped off Travis' bike. She removed her helmet, running her hand over the cap of spiky brown hair. Delighted by the results, she slipped off the leather jacket that had become hers by default.

"A lock won't keep out a determined Munch. If anything, trying to keep him out will make things worse. But I appreciate the thought."

Though Travis stowed the jacket for safekeeping, she'd held onto Meg Drake's commandeered jeans. When she knew she would meet Travis, she'd slip on the worn denim, careful to roll them up past her knees, so they were well hidden under her everyday dress.

Before she jumped on the back of Travis' bike, the dress came off, and the jeans came down.

"Then get rid of the knife."

Delaney frowned as she donned the pale-blue cotton sack. She didn't have to worry about hiding what she wore underneath since it was about the size of a circus tent.

"I feel safer with the knife nearby."

"False security, Del. If you're lucky—very, very lucky—the best you could hope for would be to slow Munch down. Temporarily. Most likely, he'll take the knife from you before you can do any damage. And if he's pissed off, he might cut you."

Travis made a lot of sense. Time after time, the scenario had played out in her head. Time after time, Delaney turned into a warrior goddess who possessed the kind of unbeatable strength and skill that only existed in the movies.

In reality, Delaney realized as she unobtrusively flexed her puny biceps, Munch could probably defeat her with the flick of one of his sausage-like fingers.

"I should've started working out in secret."

"Building up your body isn't a bad idea. But, physically, men have the advantage."

"Men have been handed most of the advantages."

Travis wrapped his arms around Delaney. So strong, yet he didn't use his superior power to frighten or overwhelm. When he touched her, she felt safe.

"You have the greatest weapon of all, Del," Travis assured her, his lips brushing the top of her head. "Your brain. Though I'm not sure cutting your hair was terribly smart."

"Do I look that bad?" Delaney asked tentatively.

"The look suits you." Travis tipped her chin upward so he could study her face. "Though you might think twice about using the same stylist."

Delaney returned his grin.

"I don't know. If the baseball thing falls through, you might consider beauty school. Women would line up for miles for the chance to have you run your fingers through their hair."

Travis held her a minute longer, neither of them anxious to say goodbye. He'd be out of town for a week. Delaney was sure Green Hills—with Travis leading the way—would return victorious. Fingers crossed, she'd win her battle as well.

"Take care of yourself," she whispered.

"If things get bad, go to my dad. Tell him I sent you. He'll keep you safe."

She knew she'd never involve Travis' father in her mess. Munch wouldn't think twice about crushing anybody who tried to keep him from what he wanted.

But to put Travis' mind at ease. Without another word, she nodded, rushing away, down the alley and out of sight, without looking back.

As the house—she'd never thought of Munch's house as a home—came into sight, she slowed to a brisk walk, taking the front steps in two leaping bounds.

Turning the doorknob, she prepared herself for what was about to come.

Alma wouldn't scream when she saw Delaney's hair. Or rant. Or curse. Her mother rarely made any sound above a whisper—or a whimper. Her reaction would mostly come in the form of a wide-eyed, horrified expression.

"What have you done?" Alma gasped, her hand flying to her mouth.

Okay, Delaney thought with a sigh. Her mother had pulled out the old horrified gasp. Her guess hadn't been far off.

"I cut my hair. What do you think?"

Silly question. Every inch of Alma, from her pinched expression to the hunched curve of her shoulders told Delaney exactly what was going on in her mother's head.

"Munch will have a fit."

"I don't care," Delaney said, a little of the confidence she felt when Travis was with her melting away. But she held her head high, her gaze unwavering. "Munch doesn't get to dictate how I wear my hair. Not anymore."

"Is that right?"

Delaney gasped, her back slamming against the closed door. Lips curled in more of a sneer than a smile, Munch stood in the hall, a can of beer in one hand. The other, balled into a fist, he rhythmically tapped on his thick, heavily muscled thigh. Dark eyes cold, they stayed glued to her, the floor creaking ominously as he deliberately closed the space between them.

"What are you doing here?"

"I live here, little girl. Lord and master. A fact you seem to have forgotten."

Munch shoved the can at his wife, beer spraying Alma in the face. She stumbled but kept the contents from spilling onto her clean floors.

Delaney fumbled for the doorknob. But she knew her efforts were fruitless. Munch grabbed her by the arm, his fingers biting into her tender flesh.

"Aren't you happy to see me, little girl? I came back early just for you."

Delaney swallowed. She didn't know when Munch started drinking, but the fresh smell of beer mingled heavily with stale whiskey.

"You've been bad while I was gone, little girl," Munch snarled. Lifting her, he slung Delaney over his shoulder, turning on his heel. "Time to find out just how bad."

CHAPTER TEN

● ≈ ● ≈ ●

"WE'RE NUMBER ONE! We're number one!"

The chant had started as Green Hills made the last out in the bottom of the ninth inning to win the high school's first-ever state championship. The exuberance had carried over non-stop for the past twenty-four hours.

Exhausted—in the best possible way—Travis rested his head on the back of the seat, eyes closed but nowhere close to sleep. They'd done what they had set out to do. They raised the trophy. In the process, Travis was named tournament MVP.

The perfect end to his high school baseball career.

Another burst of enthusiastic cheers engulfed the bus. Shaking his head, Travis opened his eyes. He could tell by the way his teammates had ramped up the noise that they were getting close to home.

"Wake up, superstar. The whole town will be there to greet the conquering heroes. They'll want Mr. MVP right out front."

Since their win, Eddie had morphed from responsible equipment manager to the life of the party. On a non-stop bender, he somehow managed to supply anybody who was interested—

which was most of the team—with all the alcohol they could want. Right under the noses of their coaches, teachers, and parents.

"Jesus." Travis winced when he got a whiff of Eddie. "You smell like a distillery. One located next to a B.O. factory. Did you bother to shower this morning?"

"Unlike you, who had time? The rest of us were too busy partying, Grandpa."

Travis shrugged, not the least bit offended.

"I partied. Had my share of beer. But since I don't like the smell of my own filth, I took advantage of the indoor plumbing in our motel room."

"Ha. Funny." Taking a long pull on the straw that stuck out of the 7-Eleven cup, Eddie sighed with pleasure. "Half Slurpee, half cheap vodka. Want some? The guys at the back of the bus call it the breakfast of champions. And lunch. And dinner."

Just the thought made Travis' stomach clench in distress.

"I'll pass."

"Your loss, man."

As Eddie slurped away, Travis turned his attention out the window and Delaney. Except when he was on the field, she hadn't been far from his thoughts all week.

Travis shifted in his seat, feeling more and more restless. The trip home seemed interminable. Was Delaney safe? Did she need him? And how long until this fucking bus finally reached their destination?

"We'll be pulling into Green Hills in about fifteen minutes," Coach Fields called out from his seat behind the driver. "Things will probably get crazy fast, so don't worry about unloading your gear. We'll take care of sorting everybody's personal possessions another time. For today, enjoy yourselves. Bask a little in the cheers and adulation. You've earned it."

"You heard the man," Eddie elbowed Travis in the ribs. "Bask. Hell, man. You won a championship. Stop looking like somebody died."

Travis nodded, but fifteen minutes seemed to take an hour. They entered the city limits, taking a right toward the high school. As expected, the parking lot overflowed. As the bus slowed to a stop, he caught sight of a bandstand drenched in the school colors. Red and gold, as far as the eye could see.

Spirits buoyed, Travis exited, waving. Some of the people had been at the tournament, but most couldn't make the trip. But they wanted to show their support, cheer their team. Thank the boys for the hard work.

Standing with his teammates, Travis scanned the crowd. He knew his father wouldn't be there. Alan had taken time off to come to the final game, but today he was back at work.

As for Delaney, Travis didn't expect to see her, but he couldn't help hoping she might have found a way to be there. Mayor Detwiler, puffed up as if he were personally responsible for bringing the trophy home, made a long, drawn-out speech before shaking each player's hand.

"Great job, Travis." Detwiler grinned, his eyes covered by a pair of designer sunglasses. "We're awfully proud of you."

Travis nodded, pulling his hand away after a perfunctory shake. The mayor waited, expectantly. Did he expect Travis to thank him? If so, they would be there a long time. Forever.

Gaze unwavering, Travis felt a tinge of satisfaction when Detwiler's mouth tightened before he moved on.

"No good bastard," Travis muttered.

The longer the celebration continued—dragged on—the more anxious Travis became. He wanted to see Delaney. To see for himself that she was okay.

Finally—almost thirty minutes later—the team was allowed to leave the bandstand. Eddie met Travis at the bottom of the steps.

"I know who you've been looking for." Voice slurred, he placed a hand on Travis' shoulder to keep his balance. "But she isn't here. I made sure she wouldn't be. You can thank me anytime."

"What the hell are you talking about? You took care of what?"

"Your wimpy little girlfriend. Delaney," Eddie sneered, hiccupping. "She tried to get her claws into you. But I cut them off. Or something like that."

Grabbing Eddie by the shirt, Travis pulled him close, unconcerned about the crowd around them.

"What the hell did you do?"

Eddie grinned, his vision too blurred by alcohol and conceit to see the burning anger in Travis' eyes.

"Contacted Munch Brill. My dad has his number," Eddie boasted. "One little call solved our problem. And put a few bucks in my pocket."

"You told Delaney's stepfather? About me? That she and I were friends?"

"Mm. Real interested, too. Hightailed it back from Mexico," Eddie snorted, amused. "Didn't like the idea of leaving his sweet little girl in your lecherous clutches."

"Fucking asshole. You have no idea what you've done."

"I saved you a lot of grief. That's what friends do."

"Friends? Not anymore. You and me? We're through. For good."

"What? Why?"

Travis wanted to smash Eddie's teeth down his throat, but he didn't have the time to deal with the inevitable repercussions. He had one thing on his mind. Getting to Delaney. Fast as possible.

He cut through the crowd, ignoring the call-outs and grasping hands. Around the back of the school, Travis didn't notice all the sets of eyes that tracked his progress. Or how several people followed close behind, careful not to lose sight.

Travis knew the alleyways like the back of his hand. He didn't have to think twice about the shortest route. As his legs carried him with the speed of an athlete—easy, automatic—his thoughts ran wild with worry. He berated himself for not protecting Delaney. Alma Brill for not protecting her daughter. And he cursed Munch Brill for the monster he was.

He couldn't rush in without a plan. Or maybe he could. He could knock on the front door and ask to see Delaney. Simple. Direct. To the point. The response he received would determine his next course of action.

Halfway there, Travis rounded the next corner. And almost smack into Munch Brill.

"Well, well, well. Who do we have here?"

Feet planted a shoulder width apart, Munch looked Travis up and down. Beside him stood a man Travis didn't recognize. But he looked like a thug. A cliché villain from a Hollywood movie. And scary as hell.

Travis took in the situation. Two against one. The odds weren't in his favor.

"I want to make sure Delaney is okay."

"I don't give a shit, you little prick."

The first swing missed as Travis ducked to the right. But for a big man, Munch was fast on his feet. The second swing grazed his chin. The third—a direct hit to his gut—sent Travis to his knees.

"Do you think you could take what was mine and not pay the price?" Munch circled. "You're lucky my uncle had his heart set on bragging up the fact his town is state champs. Otherwise, I would've tracked you down like the dog you are."

"You're scum." Travis hissed with pain when Munch kicked him in the thigh. "Delaney doesn't belong to you."

"I had the doctor check her out," Munch continued, ignoring Travis. "Still intact. Pure as the day she was born. What's wrong, boy? Couldn't get it up?"

"We didn't have sex. But we did plenty of other things."

The taunt wasn't smart, but Travis wanted to wipe the self-satisfied smirk from Munch's face. He got his wish. And another kick, this time connecting with the middle of his back, sending him sprawling into the dirt.

Silent, up until now an observer instead of a participant, the man with Munch spoke for the first time. Cool and calm. As if discussing the weather.

"Whatever you have planned, finish. I don't want my dinner to get cold."

"You think you're going to play professional ball? Be a superstar? Good luck. When I'm through crushing every finger on your fucking hands, you won't be able to pick up a fucking spoon, let alone field a fucking ball."

For the first time, Travis felt a rush of real fear. He wouldn't go down without a fight, but his best shot was to run. First, he had to get back on his feet. He didn't have time to wait for the perfect moment. Now, or never.

Travis flattened his hands on the ground, pushed up. And did something he hadn't done since before his mother died.

He prayed.

With every fiber of his being.

CHAPTER ELEVEN

● ≈ ● ≈ ●

DELANEY POUNDED AT the door, screaming for her mother. She'd tried everything. Anger. Tears. Threats. All were met with silence. But Delaney kept trying.

"I know you have the key. Please, Mom. If you don't let me out, Munch will kill Travis. You go to church every Sunday. What would God tell you to do?"

Again, silence.

After the last week, Delaney was at her wit's end. Knowing Travis was in trouble and there was nothing she could do, she felt sick—both mentally and physically—beyond reason.

The day Munch met her in the hall—home from Mexico ahead of schedule—she was certain he would rape her. Instead, he took her to see Dr. Crenshaw for an examination to determine if she were still a virgin.

Outraged, Delaney protested. She only relented when Munch gave her a choice. Let the doctor look, or he would.

The experience wasn't horrible. Dr. Crenshaw acted professionally. Quick and mostly painless. However, Delaney didn't think she'd willingly get a pelvic examination for many, many years to come.

Munch didn't say anything about her hair. In fact, Munch didn't say much at all. Back home, he locked her in her room. And there she stayed.

What Munch had told the school, she didn't know. But her meals were left outside her door three times a day. She didn't know what she would have done if she hadn't had access to a toilet. The idea of using a chamber pot was almost as horrifying as her trip to Dr. Crenshaw.

Delaney had been staring out the window when Munch knocked on her door.

"Time to take care of your boyfriend, Laney. I hope you said a nice goodbye because you won't ever see him again."

"No!" Delaney screamed, her fists hitting the door.

An hour later, her hands and voice were raw. Traces of blood marred the pink paint, but she wouldn't stop. Not even if she hit bone.

"Please," Delaney cried. "Please."

The sound of the key turning in the lock made her freeze, certain wishful thinking made her hear something that wasn't true.

"I don't know what Munch will say," Alma whispered as she cautiously opened the door.

Delaney hugged her mother, knowing the courage it took to defy Munch. Courage she hadn't thought Alma possessed.

"Thank you," Delaney gave her fierce hug.

Alma nodded, biting her lip.

"I don't know where Munch went."

"I do."

The high school, Delaney thought, racing from the house. She knew Green Hill won the championship thanks to the little transistor radio she kept hidden in her room. She'd danced around her room when she heard the news, so happy for Travis.

The announcer had mentioned there would be a huge rally at the school this afternoon. Munch would find Travis there. She only hoped she'd be in time to warn him.

Delaney took the same route to and from school more times than she could count. But she didn't remember the trip taking so long. Her legs felt like limp noodles, her feet as though they were encased in cement. With each step, she chanted to herself.

Please keep him safe. Please keep him safe.

"What's your hurry, Dippy?"

Pete Doran yelled from the corner. Miles Weller—Pete's right-hand jerk—and the rest of his friends laughed. Delaney couldn't have said why she stopped. He was a bully. A slacker. He probably got his jollies by pulling the wings off helpless insects.

However, at the moment, *why* didn't matter. She needed help, and Pete was her only port in the storm.

"Come with me," she panted, grabbing his hand.

"Sorry, honey. You ain't my type. Especially with that haircut," Pete snickered, the sycophants he ran with joining in. "Did you use a hacksaw or did you chew the ends off?"

The last thing Delaney was worried about was her hair. Or Pete's snarky attitude. Or that any other time, she would have kept her head down and avoided him at all costs.

"For once in your life, shut up and listen."

Pete's lazy gaze hardened.

"You want a slap upside your head, Dippy?"

"You could try." She'd stared down Munch. After dealing with the biggest bully God ever put on this Earth, Pete was a piece of cake. "Travis is in trouble, and I need your help."

"Now, why would I lift a finger to help Travis Forsythe?" Pete seemed to find the idea beyond ridiculous.

"Because I know you aren't a bully. Not deep inside."

Pete laughed. "What am I?"

"A hero."

"What?" he scoffed, but in his eyes, Delaney saw a flicker of something that gave her hope.

"Hear that, Pete?" Miles Weller cackled, a dribble of chewing tobacco running down his chin, mingling into a week's worth of a scruffy beard. "Dippy thinks you're a *hee*-row. She really *is* as crazy as everyone says."

"Shut up," Pete said sharply.

"A hero," she said, seeing her chance as she tried to convince them both. "Help me, Pete. Show your friends—this town—who you really are."

Desperate, Delaney tugged on his hand—this time with all her might. She'd never know what made him move. Had she magically developed irresistible powers of persuasion? Or maybe the taunt from Miles spurred him into action.

Either way, when she pulled, his considerable weight moved in her direction.

"What the hell. I ain't got nothin' else to do. Where are we headed?" he asked, chugging alongside her, his big stomach jiggling, his breathing heavy.

"I—" Out of the corner of her eye, Delaney caught a flash of red. Munch's truck, parked on the street. Near the alley. "There."

TRAVIS JUMPED TO his feet ready to run. Or fight. He pivoted, sticking his foot out, sending a lunging Munch to the ground. After that, everything happened in a blur.

Delaney rushed into the alley. Followed by Pete Doran. *What the hell*? They were the most unlikely cavalry in history, but he wasn't in any position to argue. And damn, Del looked spectacular.

Eyes blazing. Her short cap of hair a mass of wild spikes. A warrior princess ready for battle.

"Watch your back," Travis called out.

Surprisingly spry, Pete picked up an old piece of lumber and took out Munch's pal with one swing. Thunk. On the way down, the goon hit his head on the side of a brick wall. Out for the count.

Munch tried to rise. Travis shoved him with his foot. Holding nothing back, he kicked his adversary in the ribs, the sound of bones cracking like music to his ears.

"Are you okay?" Delaney asked. Out of breath, her eyes were an intense amethyst—bright with worry.

"I am now."

"I'm so sorry, Travis. Munch came after you because of me."

"Bullshit." Travis wouldn't let Delaney take the blame. He swallowed, not sure how to ask what he had to know. "Del. Did he…? Has he…?"

"No."

One word. And the cool touch of her hand on his was all the assurance Travis needed. For the first time since he left the high school, he felt he could breathe.

Delaney gasped, her grip tightening on his arm. Munch had grabbed her ankle.

"Mine," Munch ground out through gritted teeth. He tried to rise, but the pain was too much. Travis knew from experience.

Broken ribs were a bitch. And slow to heal. "You can't have her, you little fuck. Laney is mine."

Travis would have gleefully kicked Munch again—this time in the mouth. However, Pete beat him to the punch. Literally. Bending to one knee, he balled his hand into a fist, smashing Munch in the nose, producing another crunching noise, blood pouring from both nostrils.

"Sick bastard," Pete spat out. "You want me to break his arm for good measure?"

"Let me." Delaney held out her hand. With a shrug, a spark of admiration in his dark gaze—Pete handed her the board. "I think a broken leg will neutralize him longer. Don't you?"

"Knock him in the head," Pete suggested, his tone matter of fact as if he discussed this kind of thing every day. "You might put him out of commission for good."

"Self-defense?" Travis asked, just as casually. He might as well add his two cents worth. Though he didn't think Munch was worth more than a penny. If that.

Pete nodded.

"I don't think so," Delaney tossed the board as far as she could—out of temptation's way. "If we put him down, we'll be the ones who suffer."

"Mm." Pete didn't sound one hundred percent convinced. "I guess."

"Delaney has the smarts." Travis hugged her close. Damn, she felt good. "Thank you. You saved my ass. You too, Pete."

Pete shrugged, but Delaney would have sworn the flush on his cheeks was more from pleased embarrassment than any amount of exertion.

"Hear that?" Pete cocked his head to one side as the sound of sirens filled the alley. "Must have caught somebody's attention. Cops are coming."

"You can go if you want."

"Nah," Pete waved off Delaney's suggestion. "The law in this town is wonky. The more witnesses you have, the better."

Without a backward glance, Travis, Delaney, and Pete left the two men where they lay, walking out to meet the police. Two cars pulled to a stop. Luck stayed with them. Sheriff Brill wasn't driving either one.

"Travis didn't start the fight, Officer Stevens," Delaney said before any accusations could be handed out. Like Pete, she knew how this town worked. She wanted to get their side of the story told before the truth could be muddied by convenient lies. "Munch is the one you need to arrest."

"Jake," Cory Stevens nodded toward the other deputy. "Go take a look in the alley." He placed a hand on Travis' shoulder, his expression grim. "I have bad news. Your father was in an accident."

140

"Dad?" Travis felt his breath catch in his chest. "Is he okay? Where is he? At the hospital?"

"I'm sorry, son." The deputy's eyes filled with sympathy. "He didn't make it. He's dead."

CHAPTER TWELVE

● ≈ ● ≈ ●

THE HOUSE FELT wrong. Empty. Cold. As if the memories of a lifetime were sucked out the second Alan Forsythe breathed his last breath.

Alone, Travis sat in the living room and tried again to grasp what had happened. His father was gone. Dead. No mistake. He'd seen the body. Gone to the funeral. Listened while friends and neighbors offered the usual platitudes of sympathy.

The truth couldn't be denied. His father wasn't coming back.

So why didn't Travis feel...? Something? Where was the grief? The anger? From the moment he heard that his father was dead, a layer of ice had settled around him. The only crack had occurred when Delaney took his hand during the funeral. As her fingers closed over his while disapproving members of Munch's family looked on, her heartfelt concern reached past the cold—briefly.

However, the warmth didn't last. A week later, Travis wondered if he'd ever feel anything again.

"The house is mortgaged to the hilt." Davy Collins, pushing sixty, with a receding hairline and a paunch that hung over the waistband of his cheap three-piece suit, took a stack of papers from his briefcase. He was one of only three people who practiced law in Green Hills—and the only one not named Brill.

"I'm aware."

Travis was eighteen years old. What did he know about insurance and wills and probate? But what choice did he have? He had to cope. So, he did.

One advantage to a heart encased in ice? Nothing fazed him.

"Wisely, your father had set aside a little each month in case something like this happened."

"You mean in case he was electrocuted on the job?"

Davy Collins, nodded, clearing his throat. "The money covered the funeral costs. So, you don't have to worry."

"I wasn't."

"No. Well. Alan had two thousand sixty-three dollars in the bank. Taxes will take most of it. As for his insurance policy."

Travis' senses sharpened, a bit of the fog lifting when he noticed the way Davy Collins squirmed, unable to look him directly in the eyes.

"What about Dad's insurance? I know he kept up the premiums."

"Oh, he did. Yes, indeed. Like clockwork. However…"

"Here." From the box of tissues that always sat on the coffee table, Travis grabbed several, handing them Mr. Collins. "Wipe the sweat off your upper lip and spit the words out."

"The final police report states your father was responsible for the accident." Collins cleared his throat. "I believe negligence was the final determination. As a result, the insurance company has marked the policy null and void. That means—"

"I know the meaning of null and void." Travis slammed his hand down on the table. "My father wasn't negligent a day in his life. He'd never have put himself or anybody else in danger."

Fire replaced ice. Anger like he'd never known burned through Travis' blood. His father always shut off the electricity before he did anything else. Somebody had to turn the breaker back on, thousands of volts combined with the standing water in the basement a deadly combination.

Travis knew who was responsible. Mayor Detwiler's nephews. And by extension, the mayor himself.

"The money—"

"Screw the money. Detwiler. Sheriff Brill. For all I know, the entire Brill family, want to take the only thing I have left—my father's memory and reputation—and throw them under the bus? Dad isn't here to defend himself, so they make him the scapegoat."

"Calm down." Davy Collins wisely thought twice before he patted Travis on the shoulder. He didn't want to go through the rest of his life with nothing but a stump where his hand once resided. "Maybe your dad was distracted. Or upset. You don't know what happened."

"Yes. I do."

"You have a bright future, Travis," Mr. Collins said, taking a different path. "The only thing you can do is to accept Sheriff Brill's report. Your father would want you to follow your dreams. Play baseball. Have a good life. Far, far away from Green Hills."

"And what about the truth?"

With a heavy sigh, Davy Collins closed his briefcase with a snap.

"Take my word, young man. The truth—as I've learned from bitter experience—isn't everything it's cracked up to be. If you need anything, you have my number."

Travis stood on the porch as the lawyer drove away, reeling. He wanted justice. Vengeance. He wanted the truth. But most of all, he wanted his father not to be dead.

"I'm sorry to bother you. But I need your help."

A slender, slightly stooped woman stepped from the shadows. Her dark hair was pulled into a tight bun that made her fine features stand out as sharp as glass. She wore a long, loose cotton dress, socks that ended at the ankles and flat loafers. A uniform much like her daughter's.

Travis moved forward, his first thought that something had happened to Delaney. On top of everything else, he didn't think he could take another piece of bad news.

"Is Delaney okay?"

"She is. For now. But..." Alma's gaze darted around the yard and to the street. "May we go inside? Please?"

"Of course."

Once he closed the door, Travis led Alma into the living room.

"Would you like something? Water? Tea?"

In the face of Alma's obvious distress, Travis let go of his grief long enough to at least *try* to put the woman at ease.

"Nothing. Thank you."

Alma couldn't seem to settle, her hands clenching and unclenching. From what Delaney had told him, and his own assessment, Travis got the feeling the woman ran on nerves and little else.

"I'm so sorry about your father. How are you doing?"

"Better." The lie slid easily from his tongue. "You said Delaney is okay. For now? What can I do for you, Mrs. Brill?"

"Munch is laid up. You already know." Alma, eyes downcast, licked her lips. "He'll be up and about soon enough. Delaney needs to be gone before then."

Travis hesitated. He didn't know how much Alma knew about Delaney's plans. If all went on schedule, Del would be headed for Hawaii in a few days.

"He'll go after her," Alma said. "She's underage. His family has influence. She can't run far enough, not with Munch on her trail.

After the way you helped her swat him down, he's more determined than ever."

"But—"

"Until she turns eighteen, she's vulnerable. Unless..." Alma finally raised her gaze to his. "The law won't let Munch have her if she's a married woman."

"Married...?" Travis sighed. He didn't have any difficulty connecting the rest of the dots. "You want me to marry Delaney?"

Alma nodded, the dullness that lived in her eyes suddenly brightened with hope.

"If you and Laney are husband and wife, you'll be able to protect each other."

"Why do I need protection?" Travis asked.

"I overheard Munch talking to his brother. He's determined to make you pay. For breaking his ribs, but mainly for touching Delaney."

"We didn't—"

"I know. So does Munch. But you touched her. In here." Alma tapped her chest. "I watched her bloom since she's known you. Especially over the past month."

"She means a lot to me." More than Travis knew how to express—even to himself.

"Laney will never forgive herself if Munch hurts you." Alma clutched at Travis' arm, the grip of her slender fingers surprisingly strong. "The sheriff is going to arrest you for statutory rape. He'll throw you in jail until the trial. And Munch will keep Laney locked in her room so she can't testify on your behalf."

"However, if Delaney and I are married, they can't charge me with rape."

"You understand," Alma said, almost wilting with relief. "In two years, you can have the marriage annulled. Until then, Laney can live her life without looking over her shoulder."

His mind raced. Somewhere, he knew another solution had to exist. His father would think of something. But turning to Alan for a dose of wise, down-to-earth advice was no longer an option. From now on—good, bad, or disastrous—he was on his own.

"Can we even get married?" Travis realized the second he asked the question, he knew what he would do. "Delaney hasn't turned sixteen."

"All you need is parental consent." Alma raised her chin, a glimpse of her former self, shining through. "I haven't been a very good mother. I was so afraid that she'd leave me, I almost sacrificed her to that monster."

"You can go with Delaney. I know she wants you to."

Sadly, Alma shook her head. "Once. Maybe. But, I don't have Laney's strength. Not anymore. I'll live with my choices, as long as she gets away."

Why stay when she had a choice? Travis would never understand. However, like Delaney, he knew he couldn't force Alma to leave Munch.

"Are you going to marry my daughter?"

"For Delaney? Yes. Definitely." Travis nodded. "Have you asked *her*?"

"She'll agree."

"How can you be so certain?"

"She'll say yes. For you."

"YOU LOOK PRETTY. And nervous. And a little nauseous."

"You, too," Delaney said, her smile forced.

Travis adjusted his tie. He figured a man only got married once—for the first time. He should dress up for the occasion.

"Substitute handsome for pretty," he corrected.

Delaney gave him a considering look, shaking her head.

"Nope. I'd say you're pretty. In a rugged kind of way."

The fact that they could tease each other had to be a good thing—given the circumstances. They'd become engaged yesterday. Less than twenty-four hours later, they were about to say I do. Neither of them had a chance to catch their breath.

They stood in front of a little yellow house, twenty-three miles west of Green Hills, and just over the border into North Carolina where there was no waiting period—few questions asked.

All they needed were their birth certificates—and in Delaney's case, a legal guardian. Plus, the twenty-five-dollar fee for the justice of the peace.

Afraid they might draw attention if they traveled together, Travis hadn't seen Delaney since his father's funeral.

"We haven't had a chance to talk, Del."

"What is there to say?" she asked. "Either we get married, or you go to prison. End of story."

"Not exactly the romantic wedding most girls dream about."

"I—in case you haven't noticed—am not most girls."

No, Travis thought. Delaney had never been able to enjoy the flights of fancy most young women her age indulged in. She had a practical outlook that he admired. Still, today shouldn't be all gloom and doom. Del deserved something nice to look back on.

"These are for you." From behind his back, Travis handed her a bouquet of wildflowers. "I know they aren't fancy, but—"

"I didn't expect. I…" Delaney sighed, her eyes sparkling as she raised the blooms to her nose. "They're perfect. Thank you."

"They look good with your dress."

"Something borrowed and blue," Delaney did a quick turn, the skirt of the turquoise-colored dress swirling around her knees. "Our neighbor, Mrs. Thomas' contribution to the day. Your flowers are new. And I guess my underwear qualifies as old."

Travis chuckled. Though the day was hardly an occasion for celebration, Delaney could have passed for a real bride. Somebody had trimmed off the ragged bits of her hair, the curling ends held back by a white satin ribbon. Skin glowing, her cheeks held a slight blush of pink, the same color as her full, smiling lips.

Travis' earlier assessment hadn't done Delaney justice. She was more than pretty. Much, much more. And he knew he'd forever carry the memory of how she looked as they stepped up to say their vows.

The ceremony took less than five minutes—start to finish. All Travis and Delaney had to do was agree to honor each other and swear there was no legal impediment to their union.

"You may kiss the bride."

"Don't panic," Travis whispered when Delaney stiffened. "We did this before. Remember?"

Delaney nodded. She rested her hand on his chest as she lifted her lips. So sweet. So warm. Travis savored the feel of her mouth on his as he realized this could be the last time they kissed.

Travis raised his head, his arms holding Delaney's body close to his.

"Promise me two things. I'm going to send you money. However much I can, whenever I can."

"But—"

"I won't hear an argument," he said, staying her words with one finger, gently placed against her lips. "Promise you'll never try to pay me back."

Delaney hesitated, frowning. But the look in Travis' eyes must have told her he wouldn't change his mind. Reluctantly, she nodded.

"You said two promises?"

"Your bags are packed. You have your airplane ticket. Promise me you will *never* ever go back to Green Hills."

This time, Delaney didn't wait to give him her answer.

"Don't worry." When her gaze met Travis', he was reminded of deep, velvety violets. "This is one promise I will never break."

CHAPTER THIRTEEN

● ≈ ● ≈ ●

ELEVEN YEARS LATER—PRESENT DAY

DELANEY WONDERED IF her hearing had gone on the fritz. Travis Forsythe. Annoyingly handsome. Undeniably sexy. Once her best—her only—friend. Who for eleven years hadn't bothered to communicate with her unless a lawyer was involved?

This man? After all this time? After breezing in here as if he were the injured party? He actually had the nerve to pull the husband card?

"What did you say?" Delaney asked, just in case she'd heard wrong. Above all, she wanted to be fair before reacting.

"You heard me. I'm your husband, so I have certain rights."

Of all the arrogant. Egotistical... Delaney waited for her head to explode. She should be angry. Incensed. Instead—inexplicably—she burst out laughing.

Not a scoff. Of a titter. Or even a guffaw. But a full-blown, no doubt, eye-watering, belly-clutching laugh. And the longer Delaney continued—she really did try to stop—Travis turned out to be the one whose head appeared to be in danger of blowing off.

"I'd love to know what's so funny," he said, his long legs planted firmly in front of her desk, his deep-blue eyes narrowed. "I could use a laugh about now."

Delaney hiccupped, then coughed as another chuckle erupted. Her first inclination was to apologize. Which she might have done if Travis actually deserved a single ounce of atonement. Not from her, he didn't.

"Give me a second," she said, searching the top drawer for a tissue.

As usual, nothing was where she expected it to be. She'd left the organization of her office in Trina's hands. Big mistake. The teenager was great at reading while lackadaisically manning the cash register. If showing up for work each day with a different fluorescent color streaked through her hair were an Olympic sport, the girl would have nothing but gold hanging around her neck.

"Finished?" Travis inquired as he watched Delaney toss the wet tissue into the trash.

"I think so." As she took a deep breath, Delaney nodded toward the metal gray folding chair to Travis' right. "Why don't you sit down?"

When he hesitated, Delaney turned on the charm—an ability she'd acquired since the last time they met. However, if Travis looked closely, he'd recognize her technique.

The slow curving of her lips. The twinkle in her eyes. The way she turned her head a little to the side, drawing him in. Delaney had learned each move from the master.

None other than Travis Forsythe. However, unlike Travis, she wasn't a natural-born charmer.

Often, Delaney had to remind herself what to do. How to act. But not today. She'd never felt as comfortable around anybody as she did with Travis. Apparently—despite the situation—some things never changed.

This time, her smile—warm and welcoming—came as easy as breathing.

"We haven't seen each other for a long time. In case we go another eleven years, let's make this visit memorable. In a good way."

Travis visibly relaxed, his stance becoming less combative. Delaney felt a surge of adrenaline. She was in control. In charge. For once, she'd charmed the charmer. Then he smiled. Really smiled. Without warning, her stomach did a slow roll.

Travis had always been too good looking for anybody's good. When she was fifteen, she hadn't given his outer appearance much thought. They had been friends. Period.

However, Delaney was twenty-seven years old. A mature woman. She'd kissed more than a few men in her time. Welcomed a few of them into her bed and enjoyed the experience. And though

she'd wondered from time to time about the grown-up Travis—
nothing wrong with an innocent fantasy—she couldn't have
anticipated the impact of him. In the flesh—so to speak.

Was he always so tall? Or filled out? Long and lean yet
muscled in all the right places. And those arms. Biceps to drool
over. Jeans and a t-shirt never looked so good.

Oh, boy. Delaney reminded herself to breathe. *I am in trouble.*

"We were always good at talking," Travis said, his blue eyes
meeting hers. "I wonder if we could still go hours without either of
us running out of things to say."

Delaney swallowed. Finding her friend again would be so
much smarter than testing the waters as lovers. Smarter. And safer.

"We could find out. If you're game."

Travis hesitated.

"When I walked in here, I had a plan. Tear up that check, get
you back to Hawaii and me to Bermuda for a much-needed
vacation."

Delaney figured as much. Except for Bermuda. However,
Travis could tear up a million checks, the money belonged to him.
As for leaving? Hawaii would have to wait. She wasn't leaving
Green Hills. Not yet.

"You could stay a few days, Travis."

Travis frowned, obviously not enamored of the idea.

"I can only think of one good reason to stay."

Torn between curiosity and what was good for her, Delaney threw caution to the wind.

"Only one? What would that be?"

Travis took a seat, but not on the chair. He sat on the corner of Delaney's desk, his leg close enough to brush her arm as the heady scent of man reached her nose.

"My reason isn't what, but who. I'll stay. For you. If you really want me to."

Delaney's mouth suddenly went bone dry. *Tell him to go*, a little voice warned her.

"I don't want to." She'd meant to keep the thought to herself. Though only whispered, the words were loud enough for Travis to hear.

"You don't want me to stay?"

Delaney lived a safe, settled life. Not boring by any means. She was happy. Had a good job and friends she could count on. After her childhood, she'd become a big fan of safe and settled.

With one smile, Travis had stirred her up in ways she hadn't thought possible. The man was dangerous.

"Stay," Delaney said before she let herself start a list of all the reasons he shouldn't.

After all, who said a little danger had to be a bad thing?

SOMEHOW TRAVIS' PLANS had gone sideways. And he hadn't put up a whole hell of a lot of protests. All Delaney had to do—and yes, he had no problem putting the blame directly on her shapely shoulder—was bat her eyes and he caved.

Delaney's eyes always had a strange effect on him. But something had changed. *She'd* changed. Travis came to Green Hills expecting a girl. No. Check that. He'd expected to feel the same way about Delaney—the woman—as he had about the girl she used to be.

Travis liked women. He liked to look. And he especially liked to touch. To his delight, many women felt the same about him. Experience had taught him that while all women were unique, he'd never met one who couldn't easily be replaced with another.

After forty-five minutes in her company, Travis had come to a disquieting conclusion. Delaney Pope could turn out to be the exception to that rule.

As he tooled around town, Travis shook off the thought, calling himself all kinds of crazy. She was Delaney. Not so plain or simple—not anymore. She was gorgeous. Beyond the scope of how he once imagined. And then some.

However, Travis wasn't an animal. He could control his baser instincts. They would renew their friendship. Deal with why she'd decided to revisit this crap hole, and sort out the money situation.

They might even find time to touch on their marriage. A subject not high on Travis' list of priorities.

The main street seemed busier than he remembered. Booming would have been a stretch, but the amount of foot traffic milling around from store to store was a definite upgrade from when he was a kid.

Another change was the brightly colored awning that decorated the building on the corner of Main and Pine. Unlike the thrift store where he'd found Delaney, this place screamed upscale. Somebody had invested the time and money to make the outside eye catching yet classy.

Travis was proud to say—at least partly—he was that somebody.

Grinning, he pushed his way through the front door.

"Is this where I'll find the next mayor of Green Hills, South Carolina?"

A slender man of medium height walked toward Travis. Like the building, he—from his well-trimmed hair to his stylish, expertly tailored suit—carried an air of prosperity and class.

"If you can believe the polls. And my wife."

"I'll take your wife's word any day." Travis held out his hand. "Good to see you, Pete."

"Fuck that."

So much for class. Pete Doran grabbed Travis by the shoulders, pulling him in for a bear-like hug. In more ways than he could count, Pete was the total opposite of the boy Green Hills had once known. A college graduate. Successful business man. Devoted, loving husband. Doting father.

From his trimmed-down physique to his pillar of the community status. The day Pete chose to be a hero had altered his life forever.

Through fate, Pete had been on the road eleven years ago when Travis' motorcycle broke down, driving the old Ford truck he'd inherited from his father. Pete stopped and gave Travis a ride—all the way to Florida. The men had been close friends ever since.

"Last time we met you were drenched in champagne," Pete said. "By the way, thanks for winning the championship. Made taking my family cross country to Seattle worth the trip."

Travis laughed. Pete had only asked one thing in return for taking him to Florida. Tickets for all the home games the first time Travis played in the World Series. Took him awhile, but he was all too happy to pay off the debt.

"Glad I could oblige."

"Unfortunately, Emma came home with a huge case of hero worship. Seven years old and all I hear is Travis this. And Travis that."

"I don't see the problem," Travis shrugged. "The girl obviously has excellent taste."

"Mm." Pete gave Travis another pat on the back. "I could use a break from all this campaign nonsense. Let's get some coffee, and you can tell me what brings you to town. As if I don't already know."

"Another Day in Paradise?" Travis asked as they entered the spiffy little coffee shop across the street. "What was your wife thinking?"

"Candice is an eternal optimist."

"Sure. Why else would she have married you?"

The shop was doing a brisk business, most of the tables filled and a line of takeout customers waiting patiently to place their orders. Some new faces, Travis noted. A lot of old ones.

Pete waved as friends, neighbors, and supporters called out.

"Hear that?" Pete said as they took a table at the window. "That buzz is the excitement of having a celebrity in our midst."

"Shut up."

Travis was used to getting recognized. Nationally, his profile had grown thanks to endorsement deals and a World Series championship. In Seattle, as a member of the Cyclones, he could do no wrong.

However, Travis' stature in Green Hills was unique. Hometown boy made good. His return was bound to cause a stir. A fact that didn't please him.

"Should we start the countdown to your first autograph seeker?" Pete continued to tease.

Because they were friends, Travis kept his response to a low growl. On the whole, he had an upbeat disposition. Very little could get him down for long. But ever since he crossed the city limits, his thoughts had leaned more toward dark than light.

"Fucking Green Hills."

"Hey," Pete cautioned. "You're talking about my town."

"I never understood why you came back."

Pete shrugged. "During our trip to Florida? Once we started talking. You told me about your father. Until then, I'd believed the gossip concerning his death. The story I heard said he drank on the job. Came to work half-crocked."

Travis had heard those rumors. At the time, Alan Forsythe was a popular subject for the gossip mongers—fueled by the Brill family. To protect themselves, they made certain his father's reputation was reduced to ashes.

Not everybody bought into the lies. Loyal friends maintained Alan's innocence. And in his heart, Travis knew the truth.

"Power and money," A familiar flush of anger heated his blood. "The Brills never cared who they smashed as long as they kept their grip on both."

"Your father believed change was possible. Good men? Remember?"

"I remember." Travis had to smile. "Who would've guessed when we were kids that you would grow up to be so idealistic?"

"With just enough cynicism to keep from getting my ass handed to me on a plate."

"Excuse me? Mr. Forsythe?" A young boy, maybe ten or eleven, timidly held out a piece of paper and a pen. "Can I have your autograph?"

"Four minutes, thirty-seven seconds," Pete chuckled, tapping his watch.

Travis happily signed his name, drawing a huge grin from the boy. Kids were the best. In his experience, fans, in general, were great. He'd been lucky. The good encounters far outweighed the bad.

Besides, Travis knew what buttered his bread. Bodies in the seats. Eyes on the game. The day people stopped caring about baseball was the day he lost his job. A job he loved. A few autographs were a small price to pay for the privilege of doing something he loved—and paid him very, very well.

"Okay." A pretty woman with gold-streaked hair and a bright smile arrived ten minutes later, carrying a tray filled with coffee and assorted pastries. She shooed away a couple of lingerers. "Back to your seats. You got your little papers signed. Let the man catch his breath."

"Candice." Travis stood, pulling Pete's wife close. She smelled like coffee and cinnamon. "You have a unique brand of customer relations."

"They'll be back," she said, unconcerned. "This town has a caffeine addiction, and I supply them with the good stuff."

Candice brushed a kiss on her husband's cheek, taking a seat.

"I couldn't believe my eyes when I saw you." She turned to Pete. "How many times has Travis told us he'd never set foot in this town again?"

"Two thousand six hundred and fifty-two. But that's just an estimate."

"I won't be here long," Travis assured his friends. "A day at the most. But I could use a place to crash. If your standing offer is still open."

"I think we can accommodate you." Candice tucked back a loose piece of dark hair. "So, what brought you to Green Hills, Travis? As if I don't already know."

"That's what I said," Pete raised his wife's hand to his lips. "Great minds, my love. Marrying this woman was the best thing I ever did." A glint of humor entered Pete's eyes, his gaze meeting Travis'. "When are you finally going to take the plunge?"

Unamused, Travis simply raised an eyebrow.

"My mistake. You already have a wife."

"And a good one. Or she would be if Travis wises up before it's too late."

Travis frowned. He didn't like the smug look on Candice's face. As if she knew something he didn't. "Too late for what?"

"All I'll say is that Delaney might find someone who appreciates her. A man who wants to make a life with her." Candice shrugged, getting to her feet. "Maybe she already has."

"What?" Travis called out. When Candice disappeared into the kitchen, he looked at Pete. "What do you know? What man? Is there a man?"

"The question you need to ask yourself, my friend, is, after all these years, why do you care?"

Travis sat back, frowning. His reaction had been unthinking—automatic. And… telling?

Did he care if Delaney had found a man? A man she was serious about? She deserved happiness. He should be *happy* for her. And yet…

Crazy and illogical, Travis knew. But one thought kept running through his head.

Delaney can't marry another man. Because she's mine.

CHAPTER FOURTEEN

● ≈ ● ≈ ●

DELANEY HAD NEVER visited the cemetery just outside of Green Hills to visit someone she loved. She'd never had a reason—until now.

She parked near the back entrance under the shade of an old oak tree. The cool November air bathed her face as she walked down a gravel pathway, the crunch of her booted feet the only sound besides the occasional cry of a bird.

The grounds were well-tended. Green grass, trimmed shrubs, the town stretched out below a gently sloping hill. Delaney supposed the view was for the visitors—the residents couldn't have cared less. She'd never understood the fuss. If you died, a hole was a hole.

A place to visit a loved one helped some people. As a trained psychologist, she understood about comfort for the grieving. But facts were facts. Most of the graves that surrounded her, whether expensive or not, marble or stone, were long forgotten—even if the names on the gravestones weren't.

Delaney had spent years studying the human condition. At first, she took a few elementary psych classes, hoping to—if not heal—find a way to live with what had happened to her.

As a result, Delaney found a family of sorts. Friends and teachers who accepted her without question. Who admired her quick mind and helped her acclimate to a new—sometimes scary—world.

By her sophomore year, Delaney had found her vocation. She wanted to help people like herself. Children, young women, and men, who had been abused—physically and mentally. She studied and worked hard to earn her Ph.D.

Dr. Pope. The title still sounded strange to her ears. Not that Delaney doubted her abilities. She did good work and was proud of her success.

However, no amount of therapy or self-evaluation had helped her let go of the past. Not entirely. And though living forty-six hundred miles away had been a godsend, distance had become a hindrance toward taking the final step.

If she were one of her patients, Delaney's advice would have been simple and straight forward. So, she decided to follow it.

Delaney returned to Green Hills in the hope that she could once and for all exorcise what was left of her demons.

At the end of the path lay a small, tasteful headstone. As Delaney read the engraved letters, she pulled her thick, knee-length winter coat tight around her neck, knowing the sudden chill had nothing to do with the autumn air that swirled around her ankles.

Alma Christina Brill

Rest Now, Beloved Mother

The stone—a pale cream marble—and the words had been Delaney's doing. She knew if Munch had his way, nothing would mark her mother's grave—every trace and memory of Alma Brill washed from the face of the earth.

"I'll always remember," Delaney said as she knelt, her hand resting on the grass-covered earth.

"Was I wrong? Should I have fought harder to make you leave? Or should I have stayed and tried to protect you from him?"

"Your mother wanted you to leave, Del."

Delaney nodded. Blindly, she reached out, somehow certain Travis would know what to do. A second later, he knelt beside her, his hand clasping hers.

"If I'd stayed, she might be alive."

"If you'd stayed, your stepfather would've raped you and your mother would still be dead."

Just having Travis near helped. Always had. Always would.

"You always could boil things down to the pragmatic."

"I've done my share of what ifs," Travis said with a quirk of his lips.

"About your dad?"

"Mostly. And about us."

"Do we qualify as an *us*?"

Travis helped her to her feet. They started to walk and, natural and easy as the sun rising in the east, he placed his arm around her shoulders.

"We're linked, Del. I know my part in this relationship has lapsed—I take full responsibility."

"And yet I've become very close to your lawyer. We exchange Christmas cards every year."

At first, Delaney hated every piece of correspondence she received from Jacob Marks, Attorney at Law. Each precisely worded letter was like a dagger to her heart. Vivid proof that Travis no longer thought of her as a friend, but an obligation.

Little by little, the pain turned to resentment. And finally, acceptance. The regret in Travis' voice wasn't an instant healing balm. But they had to start someplace. And since he'd taken the first step, she might as well take the next.

"I could've written. Or called." She glanced at Travis' profile as they continued to stroll. "Heaven knows you were easy to keep track of. Single-A ball in Sarasota. Followed by a jump to triple-A in Tacoma. A year later, you were with the major league club. And a starter ever since. Very impressive. Meteoric, from what I understand."

Travis shrugged as if his accomplishments weren't anything special. Delaney knew better.

"The Cyclones' regular shortstop broke his leg sliding into home. Otherwise, I might have languished in the minors for years. Or been traded. Yes, I'm damn good."

Delaney laughed. There was the ego she remembered.

"However." He grinned as if he knew exactly where her thoughts had taken her. "Luck is a big part of any athlete's career. When I signed my first big contract, I held out for a no-trade clause. If I went to another team, I wanted the decision to be mine."

"Would the Cyclones have traded you? Would you have wanted them to?"

Delaney couldn't imagine either possibility.

"A lot of players would've welcomed the chance to play for a contender—something the Cyclones weren't during my early years with the team. And Seattle needed pitching a lot more than a Gold Glove shortstop with some pop in his bat."

Delaney found Travis' story fascinating. She was a casual fan of the game. But a huge fan of his. She would DVR the Cyclones—fast forwarding to when he came to the plate. Or made a play in the field. Until now, she'd never considered the business of baseball.

"But you stayed."

"I like the city. But even more, I had a feeling things were about to change for the better. Nick Sanders was brought up to play second base a year after I was promoted. Then, the final piece. The club signed Spencer Kraig. He's one of the best—if not *the* best player, in the game."

"Better than you?" Delaney teased.

"Call me a close second," Travis winked, a glint of self-deprecating humor in his deep-blue eyes.

"I read that you, Nick, and Spencer are close."

"Best friends. We clicked the second we met. Nick never misses a ground ball and Yoda—"

"Yoda?" Delaney had seen pictures of Spencer Kraig. Short, squat, and green, he wasn't.

"Everybody goes to Spencer with their problems. He's the team leader—on and off the field."

They fell into a comfortable, companionable silence. Delaney tried to think of the last time she could just *be* with somebody. When she didn't feel the need to fill every gap in the conversation with chatter.

With Travis, she wasn't worried about awkward pauses. He might frustrate her. Or make her angry. He could be arrogant and opinionated. Then again, so could she. But did he make her feel awkward? Never.

"I came back to Green Hills for three reasons," Delaney said. "First. With the help of some local business people, I want to sponsor a shelter for abused women and children. Any profit from the thrift shop will go there. Second. To support Pete. He will be the next mayor, and I want to be here when he wins. Third—"

"To close the book on your past. Once and for all."

Delaney stopped. She hoped the look she sent Travis conveyed *half* the amount of exasperation she felt at the moment.

"If you already knew, why the big hullabaloo this morning?"

"I didn't know until I spoke with Pete." Travis gently tapped her on the chin. "Unlike you, he had no problem explaining the situation."

"Did you give me a chance to explain?" Delaney tapped Travis back, with a bit more force. "I don't think so."

"I wasn't in the best of moods," Travis admitted. "Mostly? Beyond why you were in Green Hills? I was pissed about the money."

For the life of her, Delaney didn't understand why the money was such a big deal.

"I thought you would be pleased—even proud—that I was in a place in my life where I could afford to pay you back. A place where I can take care of myself. Didn't you want me to be independent?"

"Of course I did. I *do*." As he rubbed the back of his neck, frustration written across his face, Travis stared at the town below. "I wish I could explain without sounding like an idiot."

"Take the chance," Delaney playfully nudged him. "I dare you."

"Let's sit."

Travis led Delaney to a nearby wooden bench.

"I know the money doesn't mean anything to you, Travis. The amount is probably less than you've made while we've been talking. But—"

"The size of the check isn't the issue, Del."

"What is the issue? Tell me. Help me understand."

Travis nodded, gathering his thoughts.

"I can't describe how I felt the day I'd saved enough to send you money for the first time. You were my friend—and my wife— and I was finally in a position to help support you."

Delaney didn't like where he was headed.

"You considered me your responsibility? Your *burden*?" Bitter on her tongue, she spat the last word out.

Travis grabbed her hand, anticipating her impulse to stalk away.

"A burden? Never!"

"Then what?"

"Money was my way of staying... I don't know." He sighed. "Connected to you."

"The occasional letter or phone call would've served the same purpose. Believe me, hearing your voice would've meant a lot more than *any* amount of money."

"I called."

"Once. To see if I arrived safely. After that, nothing. I suppose your lawyer kept you up to date."

Without warning, Travis seemed to close up. His expressive blue eyes shuttered, hiding his thoughts from her.

"I don't know what else to say, Del. Accept my explanation or don't. The choice is up to you." Travis stood, his face averted. "If you're finished here, we should probably go. It's getting dark."

"Don't you want to visit your father's grave?"

"I had come from there when I ran into you," Travis said coolly. "Do you mind if we skip dinner? I know we had plans. Maybe another night?"

"I thought you were leaving tomorrow."

Travis shrugged. "My schedule is fluid. I don't have to be anywhere for the next few weeks. I might stay until after the election. Watching the soon-to-be ex-Mayor Detwiler go down in defeat will be sweet indeed."

"I understand you contributed a lot to help that happen. You might as well stick around and get your money's worth. Right?"

Delaney didn't know how Travis could have missed the biting tone of her words. Yet, he didn't even blink.

"I invested in the future."

"Like you did with me? Unbelievable."

With long strides, Delaney started back the way they came, determined to put as much distance between her and Travis as quickly as possible. She should have known shaking him off wouldn't be so easy. With little effort, his long legs kept pace.

"You weren't an investment as much as money well spent."

Delaney came to a skidding halt, her boots kicking up gravel.

"You arrogant bastard. Money well spent? Is that what you said?"

"You have excellent hearing, Del. I don't see any reason to repeat myself."

Who was this man? He looked like Travis. But what had happened to the sweet, sensitive man who took her hand as she grieved by her mother's grave? A touch of arrogance was one thing. But in a heartbeat, he'd morphed into a full-on jackass.

"I don't like *this* Travis." With the force of a demented game show model, Delaney gestured from the top of his head to his feet and back again. "Go away. Back to Seattle. Or Europe. Or wherever you were headed when you deigned to drop in on me."

"Bermuda," he said with aggravating calm. In fact—if she weren't mistaken—Delaney could have sworn the jerk's lips twitched.

"Perfect. Jiggling beach bimbos by the score. Enjoy."

"I plan to. But first—"

Travis swung her around, into his arms. His face was so close she could see as his pupils dilated. Delaney had no problem reading his intent.

"What do you think you're doing?" she asked, jerking her head back.

"Come on, Del. You know when a man wants to kiss you." Something close to panic flared in Travis' eyes. "*Please* tell me you've been kissed. You aren't still a—"

"Of course, I'm still a virgin, Travis. I've saved myself for you."

"What?"

Delaney must have been a better actress than she realized if the look on Travis' face was an indication. Surprise morphed into horror—another time that particular emotion might have offended her.

"Get over yourself." She shoved at him, his arms dropping without a tussle. "I'd have cobwebs growing down there if I had waited for you."

Delaney was almost to her car when Travis sprinted ahead of her, opening the door.

"A kiss wouldn't have killed you, Del. Aren't you curious? Just a little?" he asked, his effortless charm back on display.

"Maybe." What harm could the admission do? "But the grab and take what you want approach doesn't work with me. In fact, I don't think the he-man crap works outside old romance novels."

"You'd be surprised."

"Surprised? No." Delaney buckled her seatbelt. "Disappointed in you—and my fellow females? Yes."

Happy with her parting shot, she started the engine, then waited patiently for Travis to shut the car door.

"About tomorrow night?"

Why not? They still had a few things to pick through.

"If you're still here, you can pick me up at seven."

"I'll be here, but I don't have a car. I bought a motorcycle. Dress accordingly."

A motorcycle? Delaney hadn't been on one for years. Since she rode behind Travis, up into the hills. The memory of those days was sweet, and she swore she could almost feel the wind on her face.

"I'll see you then."

"Wait." Travis caught the door. "I forgot to ask. Where are you staying?"

"With Pete and Candice."

Slowly, Travis grinned as if he knew something she didn't. Something secret and slightly diabolical.

"What?" Delaney demanded, eyes narrowing.

"Nothing." So innocent butter wouldn't melt in his mouth, Travis closed the door.

Shaking her head, she put the car in drive. Five feet down the road, a thought occurred to her and she hit the brakes. With trepidation, she rolled down the window. When she saw Travis, his arms crossed over his chest, waiting, Delaney already knew. But she had to ask.

"Where are you staying?"

If possible, Travis' smile widened.

"With Pete and Candice."

CHAPTER FOURTEEN

● ≈ ● ≈ ●

"EXPLAIN AGAIN." PETE scratched his head. Why do you feel guilty?"

Travis took a sip of his beer. The bar was another addition since his days in Green Hills. With the choice of microbrews and designer labels, *Dewey's* would have fit right into Seattle's trendy downtown district. The kind of place he usually avoided like the plague.

However, Pete chose their waterhole for the night so Travis wouldn't complain. At least the tables were clean, and his feet hadn't stuck to the floor. He didn't mind a little scruff on a bar, but there was a limit.

"I don't feel guilty," Travis said. "At least, I didn't. Not until Delaney and I started down memory lane. One by one, we put our cards on the table."

"And then…?" Pete urged.

"I heard the words in my head and realized how they might sound to Delaney. How do I tell her the first thing I did when I reached Florida—less than twenty-four hours after we were married—I had meaningless, anonymous sex with another woman. Then another. And another. And—"

"Stop before I get contact envy," Pete pleaded. "In my wildest bachelor days, I never had multiple partners one after the other. Or did they overlap? A threesome? Four? No, don't tell me. I don't need another reason to hate you."

"Reasons? As in plural?" Travis had no idea. "Name two."

"Off the top of my head? You're way too good looking. And you can eat anything you want without gaining an ounce."

"I'll give you the one concerning my face." He grinned when Pete called him a colorful curse word. "Hey, the truth is the truth. However, I call bullshit on the weight gain thing. I work out constantly, my friend. And since I turned twenty-five, I watch what I eat. During the season, nothing passes these lips that wasn't approved by my personal nutritionist."

"I had no idea." Pete let out an overly dramatic gasp. "You poor baby. Life must be hell."

"Up yours, Doran."

"Back to Delaney." Pete ordered another round—good old Bud, straight from the tap. "I get why you might not want to share your sexual exploits. But why the surge of guilt?"

"I—"

"Unless you realized Delaney is all grown up. She's desirable. A friend you could tell. A woman you want? Who happens to be your wife? Okay. I get your problem."

"Except now that I've had a little time, I don't think Delaney would blame me. For some stupid reason, I panicked. And I turned into a walking, talking jerk."

Pete propped his chin on his hand with the delight of a child presented with the prospect of a new toy. "Mr. Suave put a foot wrong? This I need to hear. And don't skip any of the gory details."

"Tell me again why we're friends?"

"Because I don't blindly tell you how great you are. I give you the straight shit. Nothing held back. And—pardon my mush for a brief second—I love you, man."

"Same here." Travis gripped Pete's hand as they exchanged a bro-hug. "And by the way? You could've told me that Delaney is staying in your house."

"I could've. But Candice and I thought you would have more fun finding out for yourself. Do you mind?"

Actually, Travis liked the idea that he and Delaney would be under the same roof.

"A head's up would've been nice."

Pete merely shrugged. And grinned.

"If you think Delaney needs to know, I say go for it. But spare her the sordid details. You know. How you took one woman up against the wall. The next on the floor. A third in the shower. And so on."

"I didn't mention anything about where we had sex."

"You didn't mention an exact number either." Pete closed his eyes. "Six. No seven. Curvy blondes with big breasts."

"Down, boy." Travis had to laugh. "You realize you just described your wife. Not that I ever look at her breasts."

Pete sent him a warning look, but without much heat attached.

"Let's drink up. My dream girl is waiting for me at home." Pete took out several bills, tossing the tip on the table. "Is yours?"

"Enough already." Travis took out twenty bucks. Their waitress was five months pregnant and still managed to keep everybody in her section served and happy. For good measure, he added another hundred.

"Well, what do we have here? Date night, boys?"

Eddie Hayes. As Travis put away his wallet, he sized up his ex-best friend. Somebody had discovered the gym. A thick chest strained the material of a black t-shirt, the veins on Eddie's arms standing out in long, blue lines. Mean glinted brightly in his dark gaze.

"Cat got your tongue, Forsythe? No greeting for your old pal?"

Travis nodded. His memory was long—especially where Delaney's safety was involved. Pleasant was the best Eddie would get.

"You're looking good."

"Are you coming on to me? What did I tell you?" Eddie grinned at the men with him. Three bruisers about the same size and build. "Heard that team of Forsythe's let a fag play for them. You and him butt buddies?"

When Pete would have stood, fists clenched, Travis shook his head. He'd dealt with men like Eddie long before Cyclones' rookie of the year, Drake Langford, came out to his fellow teammates and the world last summer.

Prejudiced. Ignorant. And without a compassionate bone in his body.

Arguing wouldn't help. Fighting felt good but ultimately solved nothing. As for logic. Eddie's skull had always been too thick for common sense to penetrate. Even so, Travis couldn't resist pushing back—if only with words.

"You know, Pete? I read an article in a medical journal. Guys who constantly complain and make sick jokes about homosexuality? The ones who act as though a gay man is worse than the plague? The study found that ninety-three percent of them have man-on-man fantasies."

Eddie wasn't stupid. He immediately understood Travis' meaning. Red-faced, the veins on his arms as he clenched his fists looked like they were about to burst—as did the matching ones at his temples.

"Did you just call me a fag?"

"What I call you doesn't matter. Are you, or aren't you, Eddie? Your friends would probably be interested in your answer."

"Fuck you, Forsythe," Eddie ground out, the flush on his face turning a fiery—vaguely alarming—shade of red.

"I thought you were going to placate this asshole," Pete whispered.

"I changed my mind."

Fighting solved nothing. But sometimes, nothing felt better than pounding his fist into the face of a first-class asshole.

"You two. Hit the road."

Miles Weller, manager of *Dewey's*, didn't look happy. *Another blast from the past*, Travis thought. Former best friends to the left of them and to the right of them. *Former* being the operative word.

"They approached us, Miles," Pete said.

"*They* drink here almost every night." Miles nodded toward a smirking Eddie and his crew. "You drop in what? Once a month. Maybe? I side with good, reliable customers. Not upshot, dickwad politicians and their stuck-up buddies who roll into town thinking their shit don't stink."

As Pete's temper rose with each word out of Miles' mouth, Travis realized the situation had morphed into something out of a bad action flick. Or an equally lame sitcom. He saw himself and

Pete as the heroes—naturally. Though Eddie and Miles might have a different take.

"Come on." Travis grabbed their jackets, practically bulldozing Pete toward the exit. "You don't want to get into a brawl with the election only a week away."

Pete—reluctantly—allowed himself to be pushed out the door.

"Do you know how many votes I would get if I shoved Miles Weller's teeth down his throat? And if you knocked Eddie Hayes on his ass? Hell, I'd win by a landslide."

"Okay. Calm down, Bruiser."

"What are you talking about? I'm calm. Hell, I'm ice."

Amused, Travis watched as Pete almost shoved his fist through the lining of his jacket while in the act of retrieving his car keys.

"Want me to drive?" he asked when Pete's fumbled keys landed at his feet.

"Give me those." Pete took a deep breath as he unlocked the car. "The irony isn't lost on me, you know. I could've been one of those guys. Drinking every night. Bullying my way around town. A massive S.O.B."

"We all make choices."

"Pete the hero?"

"Damn straight."

Pete chuckled. "Who'd have thought a white hat would look so good on me?"

The friends looked at each other and grinned.

"Delaney," Pete said.

"Delaney," Travis nodded.

"Hey, pussy!"

Travis tensed, turning, fists ready. But Eddie seemed content to do his taunting from just inside Dewey's.

"I hear your girlfriend's back in town. Tell her my boss is really interested in getting reacquainted."

Sending Travis a middle finger, Eddie let the door slam behind him.

"Well, shit," Pete muttered.

"Tell me, Pete," Travis asked with admirable calm. "Who does Eddie Hayes work for?"

"You already know."

He did. But Travis wanted to hear the name.

"Tell me."

Pete let out a long sigh.

"Munch Brill."

DELANEY LOOKED AT herself in the bathroom mirror as she brushed her teeth. Face washed, hair pulled back into a neat little ponytail, wearing her favorite two sizes too big Calvin and Hobbes t-shirt. She looked about sixteen—seventeen if she squinted.

With a frown, she let her hair loose, shaking her head until the ends brushed her shoulders. The effect was a little better. Nobody would mistake her for a femme fatale. But at least she no longer looked like jailbait.

Laughing, Delaney turned off the light. The process of getting comfortable in her own skin had taken time. But she was finally at a point in her life where she liked herself—inside and out.

Trips to the gym four times a week had made her body strong. She ran three miles every day. Tried to eat the right foods—for the most part. Delaney drank plenty of water. Moisturized her skin.

Delaney Pope had come a long way in eleven years.

So why suddenly worry about how old she looked? Or how she looked—period.

I'm not worried, Delaney assured herself as she slid under the covers, smoothing a hand over the soft patchwork quilt. *Curious* was a better word. Delaney had seen the spark of interest in Travis' blue eyes.

But what did Travis *see* when he looked at her. The girl he once knew? Or the woman she'd become.

Delaney had changed. So had Travis. Her hair was longer. So was his. She had curves—hips, breasts. He'd filled out—more muscles in all the right places. So much was different and new. Including the intense attraction. A *mutual* attraction.

However, one thing hadn't changed. The connection that had drawn them together as teenagers was still there. If they were willing to provide some much-needed time, care, and attention, Delaney was certain their friendship could be as strong as ever.

As for the rest? Delaney's marriage to Travis was nothing but a scrap of paper. A legal formality that one of them should have annulled years ago. Why they hadn't didn't matter. Neither of them had worked very hard at keeping their vows.

She *did* believe they cherished each other. Love? In a way. Honor was a stretch. As for to keeping only unto themselves? Delaney snorted. Nope. Nada. Not a chance.

Eyes heavy, Delaney turned off the bedside light. One thing she knew for certain, she wouldn't solve anything tonight. For now, Travis wasn't going anywhere. Tomorrow was soon enough to start to figure out what the future held for them. If anything.

With a settled mind, Delaney closed her eyes and drifted off to sleep.

DELANEY MADE A humming sound as she felt a pair of warm lips nuzzle her neck. Almost by magic, they found the spot just below her ear that always jump-started her blood to a low sizzle.

"DEL? YOU AWAKE? I need to talk."

Mm, Travis. Wait. Delaney's eyes popped open.

"Travis?"

"Yes."

"Your mouth is doing a lot more than talking."

Delaney knew she should roll away. Or protest. Call a halt to Travis' wandering lips. But she didn't have the strength—or the desire. Instead, she tipped her head to the side, allowing him better access to all the good spots.

"You shouldn't be here."

"All you have to do is ask me to go," Travis' breath tickled her ear, a shiver coursing through her body. His hand slid up her leg, caressing the inside of her thigh. "One word, Del. Yes? Or no?"

The dark fell over them like a seductive blanket giving Delaney the courage she might have lacked in the light of day.

"You smell so good," she said, turning on her back.

Dark, but not pitch-black. Delaney could see Travis' slow smile and the intense blue of his eyes.

"And you taste like heaven." Using his teeth, he grasped her bottom lip, biting. Lightly. Yet hard enough to give her a zing of pleasure. "We can start with a kiss. I tried to take one this afternoon. I apologize. I will never force myself on you, Del."

Delaney felt a tug at her heart. Travis knew her so well. She could send him away. He'd go without protest. Or, she could take a chance and get what she really wanted.

"Yes. A kiss."

"And...?" he asked, so close his lips brushed hers as he spoke.

"Everything. I want everything."

Travis' kiss had been her first. Sweet and perfect. Innocent. But they weren't kids anymore. And the way his mouth took hers was as far from innocent as two people could get.

Delaney sank into pure carnal bliss. Long, slow, wet kisses that went on forever, Travis was content to take his time so they could get to know each other. He touched her as if they had all the time in the world.

Inch by inch, Travis pushed the t-shirt up. Past her hips. To her waist. Over her breasts.

"So pretty," he said.

"How can you tell?"

The room was dark, and Travis had been too busy enjoying the taste of her mouth to spare a glance at her body.

"I have the touch. For ground balls, and beautiful women."

Talk about your cheesy lines. And from the smile on Travis' face, he was perfectly aware. Delaney tried to laugh—to let him know she appreciated his brand of humor, but he chose that moment to cup her breast, the pad of his thumb doing crazy good things to the hardening tip.

"Holy—" Air burst from her lungs. "Travis..."

"Hmm?"

Delaney struggled to remember what she wanted to say. How could she think when his mouth replaced his thumb and his tongue— Oh, his tongue.

"We're in Pete's home. Candice is my friend. Should we do this in their guest room?"

"Where would you prefer? The kitchen?"

"Don't be silly. Of course not."

"You're right. Too public. How about the bathroom?"

Her laugh turned into a moan. Travis wouldn't be derailed from his goal—to find every sensitive, toe-curling point on her body.

"The room isn't the point."

"Pete and his family are on the other side of the house, Del." Travis sat up, removing his shirt in one fluid motion. "They won't hear us."

Gorgeous. Every rippling inch. One look at a half-naked Travis and all Delaney cared about was seeing the rest of him. And getting a taste. Her mouth watered at the thought.

"Okay," she said, placing her hand on his flat stomach. "Your skin's hot. Hard, yet soft."

"I'm hard *all* over. And getting harder by the second." Travis waggled his eyebrows. "You want to see?"

"Yes, please."

With a flick of his wrist, Travis unbuttoned the waist of his jeans. Slowly, watching her watch him, he began to lower the zipper. Just as she caught her first glimpse of his underwear, a knock sounded.

"Don't answer it, Del."

"But—"

"Don't answer it."

Delaney frowned. Travis' voice seemed to dim as the knocking grew louder.

"Delaney? Delaney! Are you awake?"

Delaney's eyes flew open to find Candice—not Travis—standing over her. Caught between disappointment and embarrassment, she rolled over, smothering her face with the pillow.

"From all the moaning, I was afraid you were sick." Delaney felt the mattress dip as Candice took a seat. "If I'd known you were in the middle of a sex dream, I never would've interrupted. We were supposed to go for a run, but I can come back if you want to finish."

"The dream is gone." Delaney was about to toss the pillow aside the bed. When she caught the glint in Candice's eyes, she changed direction, bopping her friend on the head. "You mean *finish*. As in, take care of myself? No!"

"Masturbation is a healthy way to let off steam. I shouldn't have to tell you. You're a head doctor."

"I'm pro-masturbation. But not after my friend makes the suggestion. Then pops out of the room so I can do the deed."

"Point taken. I'll meet you downstairs in five minutes." Candice paused half in, half out the door. "So, how *was* Dream Travis?"

With a groan, Delaney pulled the sheet over her head.

"That good? Can't say I'm surprised."

When Delaney heard the click of the door, she lowered the sheet.

How was Dream Travis? She stared blindly at the ceiling. *Better than any real man she'd been with.* And they hadn't moved beyond some hot, hot, hot foreplay.

Perhaps the dream was an omen. A sign sent to warn Delaney to be content that she and Travis were friends again. To stop while she was ahead. Keep sex on a subconscious level because if it turned out to be a bust, she might lose him forever.

Delaney rolled out of bed, grabbing her running gear from the closet. She tugged on a pair of leggings, a sports bra, and socks. As she tied her shoes, she ran a different scenario through her head.

What if their undeniable chemistry translated into mind-blowing sex? Why not? She certainly liked the idea. *Loved* the idea. Hoped. Literally dreamed.

As she zipped up her jacket, pulling up the hood, Delaney gave herself a mental shake. Go for a run. Get out of your head.

If she were a patient, her words would be simple. Instead of worrying, let whatever happens with Travis take a natural course. Good luck, she laughed as she jogged down the stairs.

Like most doctors, Delaney was much better at giving than taking advice.

AN HOUR LATER, Delaney felt ready to face whatever the world threw at her. A brisk run and a hot shower tended to make everything look brighter.

In the kitchen, she walked straight to the refrigerator to pour herself a glass of juice and contemplate what she wanted for breakfast.

Candice had left for work, dropping Emma at school on her way. With the election next Tuesday, Pete's schedule was jam packed. Delaney planned on spending the morning at the thrift shop before lending whatever help was needed at campaign headquarters.

As for Travis—

"I'm starving." Travis crowded her out of the way, filling his arms with half the contents of the refrigerator. "I make a mean omelet. Want one?"

Speak of the devil. Travis was fresh from a shower, the ends of his still-damp hair curling around the collar of a clean, dark-red, button-down shirt. She knew she shouldn't look, her eyes straying to the way his excellent backside filled out a pair of faded jeans. Since she was only human, she enjoyed the view, innocently averting her eyes when he turned toward her.

Delaney took a seat on the far side of the huge island. She rarely cooked anything more complicated than toast. If Travis wanted to feed her, she wouldn't argue.

She knew from watching him play ball that he had the grace of a dancer on the field. However, Delaney was surprised to see his athletic timing and rhythm translate so seamlessly to the kitchen.

Watching Travis skillfully crack eggs into a bowl, grate cheese, and chop vegetables, she almost forgot the erotic nature of their last encounter. Dream or no dream, the scene had felt incredibly real. She might have blushed—if he'd known.

Travis slid a perfectly cooked omelet from the pan, setting the plate in front of her.

"How'd you sleep?" he asked, taking the stool next to hers.

Delaney met Travis' less than innocent gaze. He couldn't know. Could he? Certain Candice hadn't spilled the beans, she shrugged.

"Good. How about you?"

"I couldn't sleep for the longest time." Travis licked a bit of cheese from his fork. "When I finally did, I was a bit… restless."

"Did you dream?" *Of me?*

"Not that I remember. Why?" As he turned his head, Travis sent her a speculative look. "Del? Did you dream about me?

"No. Maybe," she said, swallowing a delicious bite of omelet. "What did you mean? Why were you restless?"

"Because you were right across the hall. But if I'd known about the X-rated movie playing in your head, I would've been happy to give you a taste of the real thing."

With a shake of her head, Delaney placed her empty plate in the dishwasher, adding Travis'.

"Were you always so full of yourself? Or has your head expanded since the last time I saw you?"

"A bit of both, I imagine."

Delaney laughed. Damn him. Travis' ego was balanced with the ability to make fun of himself. How could she help but join in?

"Del. I ran into Eddie Hayes last night." Travis' expression turned serious.

"And?" she asked. She barely remembered Eddie Hayes.

"Eddie works for Munch Brill. He made certain I knew that Munch is keeping an eye on you."

Cold, like a shaft of ice, ran through Delaney's body. Not of fear. Those days were long gone. The most intense feelings of rage weren't always accompanied by heat. What she felt for Munch Brill was pure, unadulterated hatred.

"Every time I think about how my mother died in that car crash, and somehow he survived? He was behind the wheel. And drunk. I don't care what his brother the sheriff and a bogus breathalyzer test said."

The accident occurred on a Saturday. Munch would have started drinking before noon—as was his habit. Delaney didn't know why he and Alma were out on Miller's Road after dark, but by ten o'clock—the time the car sailed through the guard rail and into the steep embankment—Munch would have been in no condition to drive. As usual, her mother paid for her husband's disregard of anybody. This time, with her life.

"He broke his spine," Travis reminded her without a trace of sympathy.

"And will never walk again," Delaney nodded. "I hear he's in constant pain. Popping Vicodin like candy. After all the years of suffering inflicted by him on my mother? He got off easy."

Travis seemed to understand. Right now, she didn't need sympathy or comforting. She scrubbed a frying pan with barely concealed rage. Calmly—in quiet solidarity—he dried it.

"I couldn't come back for Mom's funeral." Delaney rinsed the last pan as she reminded herself through the next wave of pain-laced fury. "I knew if I saw Munch's face, I might kill him."

"Justifiable in my opinion."

Briefly, Delaney rested her head on Travis' shoulder. He'd always understood her. Instinctively. From the beginning. With a sigh, she dried her hands and finished straightening up the kitchen.

"The only saving grace is that Munch's days of targeting inexperienced, underage girls are over."

"You got away, Delaney. Men like Munch Brill hold grudges to the grave."

"Careful, you just gave me another reason to finish him off. Besides, I no longer have the two things Munch wanted from me. My youth and my virginity."

"Not funny."

Crossing her arms, Delaney leaned against the poured-concrete countertop.

"Laugh, cry, or commit murder. Take your pick."

"You have a fourth option." Travis placed his hand at the base of Delaney's back, tugging until her hips were aligned with his. "Concentrate on something pleasant instead."

Delaney went from cold to hot in seconds. Travis-fueled heat. The kind designed to make her blood sizzle in a good way.

She loved the way Travis neither grabbed nor manhandled her. He eased her toward him, leaving the final decision in her hands. Full participation or nothing at all.

"Pleasant?" Delaney leaned into his embrace, her arms sliding around his trim waist. She didn't want to leave any doubt. She was with him. All the way. "Aren't you selling yourself short?"

"Pleasant is a takeoff point," Travis said, his intense blue gaze focused solely on her. Specifically, on her mouth. "In your dream? Were we a slow burn? Or instant combustion?"

"Slow. But in a good way."

"Slow can be good," Travis conceded. "Fast can be better."

Delaney didn't wait. Ready. Eager. She met him more than halfway. She laced her fingers through Travis' impossibly soft hair, gripping the back of his head.

The kiss wasn't fast. More like wild. Expertly controlled chaos of the senses. Delaney opened her mouth with a welcoming sigh, her tongue touching his. Tasting. Learning. Exciting and heady.

"We have the house all to ourselves."

Delaney's eyes shot open as Travis bit the side of her neck, then slowly closed with a low, happy groan. *Holy crap.* She hadn't realized how good a little nip—delivered with precise expertise—would be so erotic.

"Don't tempt me."

What a silly thing to say. The man was nothing but walking, talking temptation. Head to toe. Breathing hard, Delaney didn't move as she allowed herself a moment to simply feel—to savor Travis' arms around her. A small, yet infinitely important—moment where she closed her eyes, smug in the knowledge the way his heart raced beneath her hand was because of her.

"I need to get to the thrift shop this morning. Then I can spend the afternoon helping out at Pete's campaign headquarters."

"Are we still on for dinner?"

"Yes." Delaney felt a bit reckless—the heated blood, she supposed. So, she pushed her luck. "Any chance you'll let me drive your motorcycle?"

Travis didn't laugh. Or brush off her suggestion out of hand. But his blue eyes did carry a shadow of a doubt.

"Have you ever handled a bike? They're trickier—and a hell of a lot heavier—than you'd think."

Delaney shook her head. "But I'm strong. Want to see?"

"Show me later," he said, eyeing her flexed bicep. "When I have time to give *all* your muscles a thorough inspection."

"What about the bike?" Delaney asked, following from the living room.

"No."

"But—"

Travis jogged up the stairs, pausing at the top. He leaned over the railing.

"No. Del. After you take some lessons and get certified, I'll be your first passenger. But not until then. Got it?"

"Fine."

Honestly, Delaney hadn't expected Travis to say yes. Her request had been spur of the moment. However, his response had been much better than a simple yes.

After you take some lessons. I'll be your first passenger.

Both sentences gave Delaney the impression Travis planned on staying in her life. How long and how close? She couldn't ask. Not yet. She was afraid the answer might break her heart.

One thing was certain. Delaney didn't want to lose Travis again. Maybe—just maybe—he felt the same.

Delaney snatched up her purse, exiting the house with a bounce in her step. A bounce powered by hope.

CHAPTER FIFTEEN

● ≈ ● ≈ ●

TRAVIS PARKED HIS bike outside *Reynold's Beer and Spirits*, behind a beat-up green garbage dumpster.

Parker Street ran east/west near the southern edge of Green Hills. At one time, this part of town would have been referred to as the wrong side of the tracks. Hell, for all he knew, the nickname hadn't changed; from what his eyes told him, nothing else in eleven years had.

At least not for the better.

The sidewalks—what there were of them—were little more than a series of weed-filled cracks obliterating the cement. Dangerous to navigate if you didn't watch every step.

Travis watched as a painfully thin man exited the liquor store, a brown paper bag clutched in one hand as he lit a cigarette with the other. A young boy and girl jumped to their feet and followed the shuffling man as he crossed the street.

Once, Travis hadn't given neighborhoods like this a second thought. Nor had he come so far that he turned his nose up at people who—day after day—struggled just to get by.

However, when a man with two poorly dressed children used what little money he could scrounge up for a bottle of booze and a pack of cigarettes instead of food, his sympathy was sorely tested.

The details of the man's life were a mystery. But one thing was certain, the kids—whether emotionally or physically—were the only true victims.

Travis' thoughts turned to Delaney and the shelter she planned to sponsor. Whatever she needed, he'd help. All the perks that came to him as a successful athlete were great. But he'd found the real reward for all his years of hard work was the good he could do with his money and celebrity.

Travis locked away his helmet, pocketing the key. After spending so long in Seattle, he'd almost forgotten how mild November was in this part of South Carolina. Today was a perfect example. At home, the sky would be overcast and rainy. The temperature barely topping fifty degrees. Green Hills was sunny and warm. Close to seventy with the sky a clear, bright blue.

Weather-wise, Travis was willing to concede the victory to Green Hills. In every other way, he preferred Seattle. By a wide, insurmountable margin.

One check of his watch told Travis he was right on time. After a few phone calls, he found out that Millie Charles worked as a cashier at *Reynold's Beer and Spirits.*

If she stood three feet in front of him—naked as a jaybird—Travis wouldn't have recognized the woman. However, his sources told him Millie was Eddie Hayes' girlfriend. And Eddie took her to lunch every day at eleven forty-five. Without fail. Like clockwork.

Eddie didn't keep him waiting long.

Travis heard the pickup truck well before the late model Ford came into view. Music—Beyoncé if he wasn't mistaken—blasted with pounding authority through the closed windows. Eddie always loved his music. By all that was fair, he should be stone deaf. Or well on his way.

The truck came to a stop a few feet away, the music going silent the second the engine stopped.

"Take a wrong turn on that fancy bike of yours, superstar?" Eddie asked as he exited the driver's seat, his work boots sending up a small cloud of dirt as they hit the ground.

"I need to talk to you."

Hands shoved into the pockets of his jeans, Eddie's eyes were hidden by a pair of sunglasses. However, the curling of his lip was exactly what Travis expected. Snide and unwelcoming.

Had Eddie always sported a permanent sneer—even as a boy? Or was the unflattering expression something he'd acquired in recent years. Since Travis didn't give a rat's ass, he didn't tax his brain trying to remember.

"Talk is cheap. If you want some of my time, I charge two-fifty an hour. However, for an old friend, I'll make it an even three hundred."

Travis hadn't lost his talent for solving math problems in a flash. Five dollars a second? If he thought their former friendship had meant anything, Eddie's less than subtle joke gave him the answer. As soon as Travis' reputation as a skilled shortstop grew from the borders of their little town to a wider audience, Eddie saw dollars signs. Apparently, he still did.

Pulling out his wallet, Travis took out two twenties. Forty seconds would be plenty to say what he had to say.

"Stay away from Delaney. And tell your boss to do the same."

With time to spare, he tossed the money at Eddie's feet.

Eddie grabbed Travis when he would have turned to leave.

"What the fuck is so special about that bitch?" Eddie demanded.

"Her name is Delaney," Travis hissed, jerking his arm away.

"Delaney." Eddie spit out the word. "I wish to hell she'd never been born."

"My world is a better place because she was," Travis said, never expecting Eddie to understand.

"And mine would be completely different."

"Bullshit. She didn't do anything to you."

"How many times did we talk about getting out of this town?" Arms at his sides, Eddie's hands balled into fists. "You were going to conquer professional baseball, and I would be right there by your side making certain nobody took advantage."

Travis remembered. Luckily, he'd realized in time that Eddie wanted to keep others away so he could play the biggest leech of all.

"After you became obsessed with *Delaney*, your old friends weren't good enough. *I* wasn't good enough. You changed. And not for the better."

"I'd already changed. You were just too busy partying and imagining how you would spend my future earnings to notice."

"We were a team." Eddie insisted. He snapped his fingers. "Then like that, you left me behind. In this shithole town."

"I grew up, Eddie. You didn't. You proved that when—out of spite and few bucks—you sold Delaney out to Munch Brill."

"She survived. Unfortunately."

Red colored Travis' vision. He took a step toward Eddie, intent on shutting the bastard's foul mouth.

Hitting him in the middle of the chest, Eddie gave Travis a shove.

"I'm a lot tougher than I used to be. Tougher than you, superstar." With a derisive snort, Eddie pounded his fist into the palm of his hand. "I don't have people who cater to my every whim. Clean my house. Cook my food. Carry my luggage. Wipe my ass."

The longer Eddie ranted, the less Travis felt like breaking his face. He was a little sad that his old friend had become a resentful bully with more brawn than brains.

"Actually, I prefer to wipe my own ass."

"Funny."

"I can either laugh or shove my fist down your throat."

"You think you could take me?" Eddie moved to his right, effectively blocking Travis' exit. "You won't be so pretty when I finish."

Travis sighed. Sometimes walking away isn't an option. He centered his weight and sent flying an expertly placed roundhouse kick. Eddie screamed, hitting his knees as blood spurted from his broken nose.

"My hands are too valuable to risk them on an asshole like you." Travis started his bike, strapping on his helmet. Revving the engine, he gave Eddie a final warning. "If you or anybody you know even breathes in the vicinity of Delaney, I will track you down like the dog you are."

"And to answer your question? Yes. I think I can take you."

THE MOON COOPERATED perfectly. A big, bright, golden orb to light their way. The glow added a welcome touch of warm, intimate ambiance.

Travis easily handled the curving road—so familiar despite how long it had been since his last trip up the mountain.

Everything felt familiar. The roar of the bike. The air whipping around his body. And best of all, the feel of Delaney pressed hard against his back, her arms wrapped around him like satin-covered steel.

Familiar, yet fresh as a spring rain that had washed away the bitter taste of winter. A new beginning. For him and Delaney.

Travis didn't know if Eddie would deliver his message to Munch Brill. Or if Brill would heed the warning. One thing was for sure, he and Delaney weren't kids anymore. The whims and vagaries of others wouldn't dictate how they lived their lives. They had learned to stand on their own, strong and independent. If they had to fight, they would. Without hesitation.

Independent and strong. The words perfectly described Delaney. He admired the woman she'd made of herself. However, a thought had begun to swirl in Travis' mind. A wish. A picture slowly taking shape. Clearer with each passing minute they spent together.

Delaney standing—not alone—but with him. Side by side. Together. Forever.

Logically, Travis understood he'd be smart to take a step back. He'd taken a huge leap from renewing their friendship to living the rest of their lives together. Delaney might need some time to catch up. Hell, she might run—as far and as fast as possible.

Travis had to chuckle. Delaney might hesitate, but he didn't think she'd be too surprised. Their relationship had never been conventional. Why start now?

As he turned right, Travis felt Delaney tense, her body signaling to him that she knew where they were headed. The old path had grown over, and bushes were taller, thicker than he recalled. Not that the abundance of vegetation mattered.

Travis could have found their destination in his sleep.

"Surprised?" Travis asked as he helped Delaney from the bike.

"Very." She took off her helmet. "In a good way. Are we stopping before we go to eat?"

"If you don't mind, I thought we'd have dinner here."

"A picnic. Perfect." Smiling, Delaney took a step, her foot catching on a rock. Travis caught her before she could fall. "I don't remember a rock in that spot."

"There are rocks and boulders all over the area. However, we only came here in the day, so you didn't notice."

"If I hold onto you, I won't break anything," Delaney said, taking his hand. "Added bonus? I get to hold onto you."

"I agree. But just to be safe."

Travis hit the remote in his pocket.

Strings of lights, placed there earlier that day with the help of some very good friends, came to life. Wrapped around trees. Woven through branches. Laid over shrubs and bushes. Their little getaway had been transformed into a magical wonderland.

Delaney gasped, her eyes widening, the purple of her irises sparkling with excitement. Slowly, she turned in a circle, taking everything in.

"How could you get all this done?"

"I had some help."

Travis kept his gaze on Delaney. Her reaction was the best reward he could have asked for.

"The thought of coming back here scared me. I didn't want to diminish the memories. I was afraid my mind had exaggerated the times we'd shared into something reality could never match."

"And now?"

Glowing, Delaney wrapped her arms around him.

"I wasn't wrong. About this place. Or you."

Romantic wasn't a word most people would attribute to Travis. He could be funny and a little wild. He knew that women considered him sexy. He certainly tried his best to be a good lover. And a good friend.

For the first time in his life, Travis understood how the smile of a woman could warm a man's blood. He wasn't talking about carnal heat. But a feeling that the simple touch of Delaney's hand would be enough to make a bad day better.

Travis opened the storage space on his bike, removing a basket filled with food. He spread out a blanket before opening a chilled bottle of wine.

"To new memories," he said, clinking his glass with Delaney's.

"I'll drink to that."

"Now," Travis said, watching as she pulled off her boots before stretching out her long, denim-covered legs, crossing them at the ankles. "While we eat, I want you to tell me everything you've been up to. Starting with the moment we said goodbye."

"Eleven years?" Delaney chuckled as she popped a green olive into her mouth. "Are you sure you're ready for all the mundane, boring details?"

"You do the talking, Del. I won't be bored."

More like highly entertained. Delaney's face was so expressive, her way with words so fluid, Travis could have listened to her for hours without interruption. She told him about her fears. How she'd worried about fitting in. The friends who made her transition easier. He felt he got to know each person in her life that mattered by seeing them through Delaney's incredible eyes.

"Has there been anyone special? I know you aren't a virgin."

"I won't go into details."

"Thank you very much."

The last thing Travis wanted was a graphic depiction of Delaney's love life.

Delaney sipped her wine before continuing. "I've dated. I've had several lovers. I liked them all. But no. There hasn't been a man I would classify as special."

"Candice mentioned you were dating someone."

Frowning, Delaney paused long enough—thinking hard—to allay any worry Travis may have harbored. If she couldn't come up with a name off the top of her head, he couldn't be very memorable.

"I may have mentioned Milton Ferguson," Delaney said. "Several months ago. He taught a couple of history classes at the University, and we met through mutual friends. But he was only visiting from Ireland for the semester. I haven't spoken to him since he left for home."

"Good."

"Good? You want me to be alone?"

Because he caught the teasing note in Delaney's voice, Travis wasn't worried that her life had lacked anything—socially or otherwise. He could tell she was happy. As for her sex life. He planned on doing his part to give her all the spicey good times she could handle.

"You won't ever be alone, Del. I promise."

"Don't." Delaney shook her head, the moon catching the golden highlights. "Promises are as easy to break as they are to make."

"But—"

"Tell me in a month," she cautioned. "Six months. When you're sure."

He was sure, Travis wanted to tell Delaney. He wouldn't change his mind in six months, six years, or six decades. Frustrated, he conceded she had a point. They could take time to get reacquainted. They could take all the time she needed. He wasn't going anywhere.

"What about the women in your life?"

Oh, boy. Slippery slope.

"I've known a few," Travis hedged.

"The understatement of the century," Delaney chided lightly. "From all the pictures I've seen, you've dated models, actresses, singers, by the car load. Did you ever think about settling down with one of them?"

"I'm already married. Remember?"

"Ah."

Travis didn't know if he liked her tone.

"What does *ah* mean?

"I was too busy with school. And learning how to interact with other students to think about annulling our marriage. I always thought baseball kept you so busy you forgot. Now the truth comes out. I was your safety net against ring-seeking women."

Delaney seemed to find the idea highly amusing.

"No."

"Then why are we still married?"

"Honestly?" Travis tried to find the right words. "I forgot about us—our situation—for long stretches of time."

"Flatterer."

"Come on." Travis gave Delaney's leg a shake, then, because he liked touching her, left his hand where it was. "I don't believe I was on your mind twenty-four hours a day."

"Of course not. But I never forgot you."

"I used the wrong word." Travis tried again. "You were tucked away. In storage—so to speak."

Delaney laid her hand over his. And the gesture felt natural. Right.

"Better," she said.

"I could've arranged an annulment any number of times. Something so quick and emotionless never felt like the way we were supposed to end. Does that make sense?"

"To me? Yes." Laughing, she lay on her back, keeping hold of his hand. "Our story isn't an easy one to explain. Crazy, some might say. Here we are. Back where we started. Yet each of us has come so far."

"You like who you are?" Travis asked.

Delaney nodded.

Propped on his elbow, Travis leaned over her. As he cupped her cheek, her smile widened, and her eyes grew so dark the purple bordered on black.

"I like who you are, Del. I always have."

"Have you ever wondered why we click so seamlessly? Back then? Now? On paper, we should be like oil and water."

"On paper." Travis had to laugh. "Almost a year ago, months before the season started? The Cyclones were picked to win the World Series."

"And you did."

"True. But as my buddy Spencer Kraig pointed out, there's a reason why we play a hundred and sixty-two games. Predictions mean about as much as the paper they're written on. At one point during the season, we struggled. Mightily. Our hopes of a championship were close to going off the rails."

"How did you fix the problem?"

"The Cyclones are a diverse group. Different cultures. Different beliefs. *On paper*, we shouldn't work. But I love those guys. Every single one. We faced the problem. Together. Believed in each other. I know for a fact we came out the other side stronger than ever."

"I always believed in you." Delaney turned her head, her lips brushing the palm of his hand.

"We fit." Travis leaned closer. "Perfectly."

"I agree."

Travis wanted to give Delaney romance. Their first time. Sweet, gentle, loving. He hadn't expected the burst of passion that exploded the second his mouth touched hers.

The thought that he should pull back, take a breath, slow things down, flashed through his brain. And he might have managed, except Delaney made her feelings clear from the start. She wasn't interested in sweet or gentle. Wild, molten-hot sex was on her agenda.

And Travis was more than happy to comply.

"Shirt. Off. Now."

In a flash, Travis sent his shirt flying. The night did nothing to cool the heat of Delaney's eager touch.

"You next."

Delaney raised her arms. He couldn't resist smoothing his hands up her back as he raised the cloth inch by inch. She sighed with pleasure, and the sound was like a high-octane aphrodisiac.

Shirt. Bra. Half-naked Delaney. Her skin, like alabaster, shimmered in the moonlight. Smooth. Soft. Travis couldn't get enough.

"Kiss me." Delaney wiggled her eyebrows. She ran a finger down her throat, stopping at the slope of her breast. "Here."

Travis was more than happy to let Delaney drive the action—for now. Especially when she steered him in all the right directions.

Delaney gasped.

"I didn't tell you to use your tongue."

"Any objection?" Travis punctuated his question by lapping at her nipple.

"Nope." She threaded her fingers through his hair, the tips contracting when his teeth joined the fun. "Please, carry on."

An excellent multitasker, Travis disposed of the rest of his clothing in quick order. Delaney's followed. She had the legs of a dancer. Long, lean, shapely. He wanted them wrapped around him, urging him on.

"Please."

Delaney sounded desperate. And Travis was right there with her. He fumbled with his jeans, letting out a sigh of relief when he found the condom on the first try.

"Better than your dream?" he inquired, settling between her spectacular legs.

Licking her lips, Delaney frowned, her eyes a sparkling amethyst.

"What dream?" she sighed.

"Mm. Good answer."

Travis entered her with one push. The glide easy. Their bodies were made for each other. A perfect fit.

Breathing heavily, Travis watched the emotions race over Delaney's face. Marveled as the color of her irises deepened. She arched her neck, air bursting from her lungs. So close. He could tell by the flush of her skin, the tightening of her legs as they twined around his.

"Now," Travis said, needing her to fall with him.

"Now!" Delaney called out.

Reaching up, up, up. Then bursting through. Skyrockets. Travis was certain he saw a whole rainbow of colors. Over and over they fell. Tumbling down, the descent much slower than the rise.

Travis collapsed, rolling to the side, keeping Delaney safely tucked in his arms.

He felt Delaney's lips graze his chest before she snuggled close. Limp, but satisfied.

The stars and the moon blanketed them. Somehow, the light seemed brighter. More intense. As if, after serving as witness to something beautiful, the sky wanted to show its approval.

"Are you cold," Travis asked.

"No. Just right. Practically perfect."

Travis rested his hand on Delaney's hip. Practically perfect. He liked that. They might never reach perfection. He didn't care. But wouldn't they have fun trying? Over and over and over again.

CHAPTER FIFTEEN

● ≈ ● ≈ ●

"ARE YOU SURE about this?"

"Positive."

"I don't want to abuse your trust."

"I don't think you could." Travis kissed Delaney before sitting on the chair placed in the middle of the back deck. "Besides, you trusted me."

The situation was completely different, as Travis knew. He chopped off her hair in a show of unified defiance. She hadn't cared about how the end product looked.

"How much do you usually pay for a haircut?" she asked, settling a towel around his shoulders.

"From anybody else, I would find a question about how much I pay for anything extremely rude."

"How much?" Delaney prodded, unconcerned. Her curiosity was piqued.

"Five hundred."

"Dollars! Who are you? JLo?"

"Some of my teammates pay double. Of course, they get highlights put in and deep-scalp treatments."

"For the love of..." And men complained that women were vain. "Too much money, too few brains."

"You have the scissors. I don't argue with anybody wielding a deadly weapon."

"You don't argue because you know I'm right."

Last night in bed, Travis mentioned he needed a haircut. Delaney didn't agree. She liked the way the ends curled around her fingers as if they didn't want to let her go. But she'd admit his hair was a bit on the shaggy side. Some shaping and an inch or two shorter.

Travis wasn't thrilled at the idea going to a local salon—or barbershop. Delaney's mistake was teasingly offering to do the job herself. Once she'd put the idea in his head, he was like a dog with a bone. Good luck getting the thing away from him.

"You'll want to look your best since today is Election Day. Don't you want somebody with a little more experience?"

Or with any experience at all?

Between Delaney's junior and senior years of college, she had a job sweeping up hair at a beauty parlor—the down-to-earth owner of *Ms. Jones' Clip, Snip, and Color* didn't consider her place highbrow enough to be called a salon. When things were slow, Ms. Jones would give Delaney lessons using an old wig.

Delaney quickly discovered that hairdressing wasn't her calling.

"First. I'm not the one running for office. Second. I have complete faith in you. Besides, hair grows back."

"Ears don't," Delaney muttered.

Travis laughed. He actually *laughed*. Delaney didn't know if that was a good sign for her nerves, or not.

"My advice? At the first sign of blood, stop cutting."

Breathing in, Delaney, took a lock of damp hair and snipped. Then another. And another. As hair piled up at her feet, her confidence grew. She went a little shorter than planned because she had to even out one side then the other.

And, she might have finished sooner if Travis had kept his hands to himself—though she did like that he couldn't stop himself from touching her.

Not bad, Delaney decided, standing back to admire her work. Not bad at all. She wouldn't turn in her psychiatry license anytime soon. Still, in a pinch, she knew she could cut hair, be proud of the end results—and not draw even a fleck of blood.

"Want to look?"

Delaney held out a mirror.

"And you said you didn't know what you were doing." Travis admired her handiwork. "I'd pay you five hundred without blinking."

"Stop exaggerating." Though Delaney was pleased by his response. "You have great hair, and I didn't cut off anything vital. Let's stop there."

Taking the towel, she shook the excess hair into the garbage. She picked up a broom and swept up the rest. As usual, Travis was more hindrance than help in the clean-up department. However, when his arms wrapped around her, his chest pressed against her back, she could have happily labored away for hours.

"Add a kiss to the cut. You could double your fee."

"I could get rich. Should I advertise my services to the public?"

"Private." Travis tossed aside the broom, twirling her to face him. "Just you and me."

When Travis kissed her, the world ceased to exist. Delaney wanted to believe in forever. Though she'd asked him not to make any promises, he told her how he felt again and again. Every look. Every touch. They were all her dreams come true.

Unwanted doubts kept creeping into Delaney's thoughts. Would Travis be happy if he gave up his bachelor ways? To exchange a different woman every night for only one? She wanted him to be sure. But how?

Delaney had an idea. And she knew Travis wouldn't approve. In fact, she was almost certain he'd blow his top.

To truly know if they belonged together, Delaney had to set Travis free.

"LADIES AND GENTLEMEN." Pete tapped on the microphone. The crowded lodge—courtesy of the Elks—quieted to a low buzz of anticipation. All evening, they had monitored the election results. The excitement had built with the news of the first returns.

All Pete's supporters needed to celebrate were the words they knew were coming.

"I just received a phone call from my *worthy* opponent."

"Boo! Down with Detwiler. Hayes all the way."

"Don't you love how politics brings out the best in people?" Travis said to Delaney. They stood to one side of the stage, watching with pride as what had become the inevitable played out.

"Horace Detwiler has conceded the election." Pete paused, hugging a beaming, teary Candice close. "We won!"

The eruption could have rivaled a volcano—a small, jubilant one.

A server with a tray of champagne passed by, Travis snagging a couple glasses.

"To Pete."

"To a new and better Green Hills."

Just before Pete made his announcement, word had come down concerning another hotly contested race. A new sheriff was in town. The job one Brill family member or another had a strangle hold on for what seemed like forever, was now in the hands of Tonya Hernandez—a fellow graduate of the local high school who believed she could make a difference.

The Brills' iron grip had been broken. A new generation with no old-boy ties was now in charge.

"Dad once told me that change could happen if good men—and women—were willing to put up a fight." Travis' voice thickened with emotion. "I wish he was here to see Pete and Tonya and all these people prove him right."

"Don't leave yourself out. Your dad would be proud of how much you did to help Pete win."

Delaney hoped—wanted to believe—Travis' father could see the man his son had become. She hoped her mother was up there with Alan Forsythe. Finally free. Finally at peace.

"*We* helped. Everybody in this room did their part." Travis tipped her chin up a few inches for a lingering kiss. "But Pete is the miracle worker. He made this town believe in him and a better future."

"Go on and congratulate him." Delaney pushed Travis toward the stage.

"Aren't you coming?"

"I'll be along as soon as I use the bathroom. Hopefully, everybody is too busy celebrating to wait in line to take a pee."

"Maybe I should go with you?"

"Because…?" As far as Delaney was concerned, what she had to do was best done with as much privacy as possible.

"The Brills lost a lot of their power today. They're wounded, but they aren't dead yet. If they—Munch in particular—decide to lash out in frustration, you could be a target."

Delaney was used to keeping her guard up. Even in Hawaii, she'd worried that Munch might try something. Slowly, she relaxed. But she was always aware of her surroundings—especially since her return to Green Hills.

"I'm surrounded by hundreds of people. I don't think the Brills would have the balls to try anything."

"Del—"

"However." Because she understood—and appreciated—Travis' concern, she wanted to reassure him. "I will be careful. Always."

The line for the ladies' room was long—surprise, surprise. The men's room—naturally—not so much. Resigned, Delaney took her place.

"I need to talk to you."

Cletus Brill grabbed her arm. His eyes were bloodshot, his breath reeked of whiskey—both fresh and stale.

"Take you hand off me, Cletus."

"I got something to say."

The fact that he'd been drinking was obvious, but Delaney didn't think Cletus was drunk. His speech wasn't slurred, and he seemed steady on his feet. He hadn't aged well. She estimated his age to be near forty. He looked ten years older. At least.

"Then talk."

"In private."

Maybe Cletus wasn't drunk. However, the man was downright crazy if he thought Delaney would go anyplace with him.

"Go home, Cletus."

"Please." Tears filled his eyes. "I've been living in hell for so long. I need some peace. I need to confess."

"About what?"

"What we did to Travis Forsythe's daddy."

TRAVIS LOOKED AROUND the room. He'd decided to give Delaney ten minutes. The minute hand on his watch just passed fifteen. Heading toward the bathroom, he knew she'd tease him for worrying too much. But he didn't care.

If anything happened to Delaney, his life wouldn't be worth living.

The bathrooms were on the other side of the hall. Getting there became an exercise in frustration. The party was in full swing. Dancing. Drinking. A few people had lost all inhibitions, making out like rabbits right in front of anybody who cared to notice.

Travis had barely dodged, pushed, and maneuvered halfway to his destination when he heard his name.

"Travis."

"Delaney." He held her close. "Thank goodness. I felt like a salmon swimming upstream."

"Travis." Delaney held him tight for a second longer. When she touched his cheek, her eyes were the color of muted violets. "Come with me. You need to hear something."

Puzzled, Travis followed her, hands linked, to a door hidden by a bank of sound equipment. His confusion didn't clear when he saw who was waiting for them.

Pete. Sheriff Tonya Hernandez. And— Son of a bitch. Why would Delaney take him to see Cletus Brill?

"Don't look at me," Pete said. He'd long ago lost his suit jacket. His sleeves were rolled up to his elbows, tie slightly askew, a slight trace of his wife's lipstick clinging to the corner of his mouth. "Delaney said we had to be here. So, here we are."

Tonya Hernandez wasn't an imposing woman—at first glance. But the ex-Army staff sergeant had a demeanor that could cut a person twice her size to his knees with a single glance.

"I was dancing with my husband—something we don't get to do very often." The new sheriff shot a look Delaney's way that said, *whatever this is, it better be good.*

"I appreciate you coming so quickly. I know tonight is for celebrating. But Cletus Brill has some information all of you need to hear." Delaney squeezed Travis' hand. "About the murder of Alan Forsythe."

Travis stiffened. What the hell? *Murder*? Delaney nodded, her expression filled with concern and sadness.

"Cletus? Tell everybody what you told me."

"I—" Cletus' gaze darted around the room, looking everywhere except at Travis.

"Say what you have to say. I won't hurt you," Travis assured the profusely sweating man. *Not right away.*

"The day your daddy..." Cletus swallowed hard, wiping his upper lip. "That day, me and Myron were late. I guess we always were. We'd been drinking—not your daddy. He never. He was a good man."

"I thought you were here to tell me something I don't know."

Hearing Cletus Brill praise his father seemed like a sick joke. The Brill twins had been at the forefront of tearing down Alan Forsythe's reputation, spreading lies as fast as wildfire. Now? Eleven years later, Cletus had changed his tune? *Fuck that.*

"Go on, Cletus," Delaney urged, in a calm, soothing voice. Doctor mode, Travis supposed. "You finally want to tell the truth so you can find some peace of mind. Remember?"

"Right. Right." Cletus took a seat, the plastic chair groaning under his considerable bulk. "Myron said it would be a joke. A huge laugh. Shock Mr. Forsythe. That's all. We'd flip the electricity on."

"Oh, my Lord," Tonya Hernandez gasped.

"A little shock. That's what Myron said. I swear I didn't know your daddy would die. I swear. I swear."

Head in hands, Cletus repeated the words over and over, his tears hitting the floor.

"Travis. Don't."

Delaney must have felt his muscles tense—bunched—ready to spring. Ready to destroy what was left—the hollowed-out shell— of Cletus Brill. Travis' instincts told him to act. His free hand formed a fist. His blood ran hot with the need for revenge.

Then what? Travis felt as much as heard his father's voice. At best, he'd feel a temporary satisfaction. Drawing blood wouldn't bring Alan Forsythe back. Or dull the pain. The truth hurt—like a sucker punch to the gut.

At least he knew. And so would everybody else. Travis would make certain.

"What about Myron?" Once he could take a steady breath, Travis needed details. "Did he know my father would die?"

"Yes."

"Why?" Pete asked. "What possible reason could your brother have to kill Alan Forsythe?"

"Uncle Munch asked him to."

Delaney gasped, her eyes wide with horror, she looked at Travis. *I didn't know*, she mouthed. When she tried to pull her hand away, Travis held tight.

"Wipe that guilt from your face, Del."

"But—"

"Not. Your. Fault."

Travis wouldn't let Delaney take on an ounce of the burden. Munch Brill was a monster. And he'd pay.

"You need to arrest Brill. Immediately."

"I don't have the authority," Tonya said. "Until I'm sworn in, Sheriff Brill is in charge."

"So, we have to wait until January?"

Travis could live with Brill behind bars. But if the bastard was allowed to breathe free air one more day. Or worse, skip town? He didn't know what he'd do.

Though he wasn't an expert criminal, Travis didn't think he'd have too much trouble figuring out where to hide Munch's body.

"Are you willing to make a formal statement?" Pete asked Cletus.

"Yes. Whatever. I'll do whatever you want."

"The timing could be tricky." Tonya frowned, considering their options. "If we can catch all the players in one place, they won't be able to circle the wagons in time. The sheriff won't have any option but to arrest Munch."

"They'll be licking their wounds." Travis wanted in. Tonight would be the end. The final chapter. He wanted to be there when Taps sounded for Munch Brill. "*Dewey's?*"

"Cletus?" Pete asked.

Nodding, Cletus wiped at his wet cheeks. "They're all at Dewey's."

"I'll call in the officers I know we can trust." Tonya was already on her phone. "In the meantime, we get Cletus' statement on record. Signed and sealed. Delivering will be a pleasure."

The next hour felt like ten. Finally, Pete and Tonya agreed they had what they needed. A notarized document and the manpower to make their move.

"Before you ask, you can't come," Pete told Travis. "We have to do this by the book."

"Fine."

"Really?" Pete looked skeptical.

"If I can't ride with the big boys, I'll simply head to the bar on my own."

"*We'll* head to the bar."

Delaney raised her chin, daring Travis to contradict her. After everything they'd been through—where they were today—he wouldn't have dared. As much as anyone, she deserved to see justice done.

"You heard the lady."

"Fine," Pete grumbled as he pulled on his jacket. He'd learned a long time ago what was worth a fight and what wasn't. "Do me one favor?"

Travis waited, unwilling to commit. He'd hate to lie—he would if he had to—but the process wouldn't make him feel good.

"If you end up killing Munch Brill? Make certain there aren't any witnesses."

THE PARKING LOT outside *Dewey's* was full. But unlike the crowd at the Elks, nobody was celebrating.

Surprisingly, Delaney felt calm. Almost Zen. She could have credited her education. All the psychology courses. The extensive training. Theoretically, she was well prepared to take on any and all demons from her past. Unfortunately, too often, reality obliterated theory.

Delaney's lack of nerves had nothing to do with what she'd learned in books. The difference between now and eleven years ago was that this time, people had her back. A solid wall of defense she could count on not to crumble.

"You okay?" Travis asked.

"Yes. You?"

"Been a hell of a day."

They stood back as the police entered *Dewey's*, led by Tonya. Pete went next. Delaney and Travis agreed to enter last. Out of the line of fire—so to speak.

"All I ever wanted was to see Munch pay. A broken spine never seemed enough." Delaney looked up, thinking of her mother. "He'll probably die in prison, Travis."

"Probably."

"How does that make you feel?"

"Are you asking as a head shrinker or as my friend? My lover?"

"I am who I am." Delaney understood why he asked. "However, first and foremost, I'm your Del."

"You are that." With a sigh, Travis touched her cheek. "I want Brill locked away for good. Then? I want *us* to live free. And forget he ever did."

"Amen."

"This is a private party, *Mr. Mayor*." Miles Weller eyed Pete with contempt, his gaze flickering with concern when he spied Tonya Hernandez and the six police officers flanking her. "What the hell is going on?"

"We need to speak with the sheriff and the mayor," Pete said.

"Brill and Detwiler," Tonya added.

"Kind of confusing. Too many mayors and sheriffs for anyone's good," Miles snorted. "What the hell. This place could use some livening up. You'll find the mourners over at the bar."

Frowning, Delaney hung back, scanning the room. Her problem wasn't with what she saw, rather what she *didn't* see.

"Something wrong?" Travis asked.

"Where's Munch?"

"Right behind you, little girl."

Facing the devil was a daunting prospect. Even when his power to do evil had been neutralized. The mind was a powerful thing. Delaney knew Munch couldn't hurt her. Yet—for one brief moment before she turned to face him—she felt like she was fifteen with no friends and little hope.

Then, Delaney remembered. She got away. She beat the devil.

Munch's only victory was the hold he'd had on her mother. In the end, a hollow victory. Alma could have left. She *chose* to stay. Her chains had been forged from fear, not steel.

Delaney had come to the realization that her mother had always been scared of ending up alone. She'd never recovered from her first husband leaving. She needed to be somebody's wife. Even if that somebody mentally and physically abused her.

In a bit of twisted irony, Munch was the one who ended up alone. No wife. No *little girl*. Soon—as the seconds ticked by—not even his family would be there to cover up his crimes.

Delaney met Travis' ice-blue gaze, nodded, and then turned to face the devil.

Munch was in a wheelchair. His once powerful body withering—almost caved in on itself. Bitterness etched into his face. *Almost pathetic*, Delaney thought. If she could have dredged up an ounce of sympathy.

"Shame on you for not visiting your step-daddy sooner. We have so much to catch up on. Here." Leering, Munch patted his lap. "Climb on. Remember how much fun we used to have?"

"You sick son of a bitch." Travis ground out.

Delaney hadn't noticed Eddie Hayes from where he stood behind Munch. Attendant? Bodyguard? Whatever his job, he stepped in front of the wheelchair, crossing his arms.

"Keep back, Forsythe," Eddie warned, a white bandage covering his bruised, swollen nose.

"How can you work for this piece of scum? What the hell happened to your pride? Your sense of right and wrong?"

"Fuck right and wrong. And fuck you." Eddie gave Travis a shove. "You were lucky the other day. Next time, you'll be the one on the ground. And you won't get up."

"And you said you ran into a door," Munch cackled.

He seemed to find the entire situation amusing. The light in his eyes bordered on crazy—not a word Delaney liked to use in a professional capacity. But in Munch's case, crazy fit. She wondered how much humor he would' find when they slapped a pair of cuffs on him and wheeled him off to jail.

"Travis." Delaney reached for his hand, tugging. She had as much luck as if she had' tried to move a column of forged iron. "Please. Let Pete and Tonya do their jobs."

"He killed my father," Travis said, more to Eddie than to her.

Delaney thought she saw some kind of emotion flicker through the cold in Eddie's eyes. Sympathy? Regret? Too brief for her to identify, the moment passed. And for Travis' sake, she was sorry.

"I've done a lot of things in my day," Munch smiled as if savoring the memory. "Killing Alan Forsythe wasn't one of them."

"You deny telling Myron Brill to electrocute Travis' father?"

Arrogant to the last. So certain nothing and no one could touch him, Munch shrugged.

"Sure I did. But technically, I didn't do the deed."

"Why?" Anger at her or Travis was one thing. But to willfully take another life? "What reason could you possibly have?"

"Your boyfriend took something from me. Something precious. So…? Tit for tat, little girl."

Delaney had no words. If Travis had wrapped his hands around Munch's throat, she wouldn't have blamed him. She didn't know if she would have intervened. Luckily, she didn't have to find out.

Travis didn't blink. Or move. The contempt in his eyes was lost on Munch, but Delaney saw. Strong, courageous. Unlike her stepfather, he didn't prey on the weak—no matter how deserving his wrath.

He could have hated her. Blamed her by association. But he didn't.

Travis Forsythe was more of a man—a human being—than anybody she had' ever known. And she loved him with her entire heart, body, and soul.

"Prison is too good for you," Travis said. "But a jail cell will have to do for now."

"Prison?" Munch scoffed. "I'm a Brill, boy. And this is Green Hills. Nobody will ever take me down."

"Times have changed."

Delaney pointed across the room just as Tonya handed one copy of Cletus Brill's statement to the sheriff and one to the mayor. As they read, a layer of arrogance slipped.

Before they left for Dewey's, Tonya put in a call to the head of the state police, outlining the situation. For good measure, Pete called the governor. Copies of Cletus' statement were now in the hands of people who had no ties to Green Hills—professionally or personally. A new generation. People who weren't under the Brill's thumbs and influence.

Sheriff Rick Brill. The man who'd spent most of his life cleaning up his brother's messes sent a brief glance Munch's way. And shrugged.

"Your luck has just run out, Munch," Travis said as two uniformed officers approached.

Reality finally penetrated Munch's delusional brain.

"Eddie! Get me out of here."

"Sorry boss." Hands in the air, Eddie slowly backed away. Money could only buy so much loyalty. "Sorry, boss. I don't take a bullet for nobody."

"Munch Brill? You're under arrest for the murder of Alan Forsythe."

"No!" Munch struggled, but the officer had little trouble cuffing his wrists. "Rick! Uncle Horace! Somebody make them stop! Tell them. I don't go to jail. I'm a Brill, damn it."

Delaney didn't watch as Munch was taken away. She was done. She never wanted to see the man again. Travis took her in his arms, holding her close.

"Justice."

"Yes," Travis said.

The end of Munch Brill was a little bittersweet for both of them. They missed their mother and father. Always would. However, they'd done their grieving.

The best way to honor their parents would be to move on. To be happy. To live.

CHAPTER SIXTEEN

● ≈ ● ≈ ●

"I WON'T be there for Thanksgiving. I plan to stay here in Green Hills until after the holiday."

Travis heard the words come out of his mouth, shaking his head. For a man who had once sworn never to set foot in his home town again, he couldn't believe he had' been here three weeks. Pete and Candice had issued a standing invitation to visit any time he wanted.

And the crazy part? Travis knew he would be back.

"A lot has happened since the last time we saw each other," Spencer Kraig chuckled. "I'm glad you called and caught me up."

Spencer was the best sounding board Travis knew. Instinctively, the Cyclones' third baseman knew when to simply listen, or when a friend needed his advice. At the moment, Travis needed the latter.

"Green Hills used to be my home. A place I belonged. Where I felt safe. Welcome. I haven't felt that way since Dad died."

"Hometowns have a powerful pull. As do first loves."

Spencer was engaged to Blue O'Hara. The love of his life—his first love. They found each other again. A true happily ever after.

After a whole bunch of heartache. Travis and Delaney's situation wasn't the same.

"Del and I were friends. Married in name only. I wasn't her first love. She wasn't mine."

"From what you've told me, I think you're wrong," Spencer said. Three thousand miles away and he still saw things clearer than Travis could. "You loved each other, whether romantic or not. The years apart didn't change anything. Except now Delaney is a grown woman. You've *both* grown."

Spencer was right. As usual. Even if Travis had been in love with Delaney—the way a man loves a woman—he hadn't been ready for her. And she certainly hadn't been ready for him.

They had lived apart. Experienced different things. Had friends and lovers. All the while, the connection between them had never broken. Somehow, they found their way back. To Green Hills. And to each other.

"I've come to terms with my hometown. But Seattle is the only place I can see myself long term."

"What about Delaney? Can you see yourself with her—long term?"

"Yes." Travis didn't hesitate. He knew what he wanted. *Who* he wanted. "I think she feels the same."

"But...?"

"Something is holding her back." And frustrating the hell out of him. "We talk about everything. Non-stop. But she won't let me even mention the future. For some reason, she thinks I'll change my mind."

"Okay."

"Excuse me? I called you because you always have an answer. I need more than okay."

"Ask yourself one question. You've waited this long. Is Delaney worth a little more time? What could turn out to be a truckload of patience?"

Again, Travis didn't need to think.

"For Delaney? Anything."

"Good answer, my friend. I've been there. Take my word. Slow or fast. Tomorrow or a year down the road. A woman—the *right* woman—is always worth the wait."

THE HEADY FRAGRANCES of Thanksgiving filled the house. Travis paused in the hall to breathe in. Turkey. Homemade dinner rolls. Mashed potatoes. And pie. Pete—of all his accomplishments, baker was the most surprising—concocted three different kinds. Pumpkin had Travis' name all over it.

He'd always been a fan of the food—even when he felt he had little to be thankful for.

This year, everywhere Travis looked, the blessings overflowed. If he were the suspicious type—the kind of person who thought too much of a good thing was just asking for trouble—he might worry that things were going too well.

Munch Brill was in prison—charged with Alan Forsythe's murder. Despite Brill's continued assertion that he'd go free, all signs pointed toward a conviction.

Cletus Brill—sober as a judge since making his statement—stood by his story. When faced with the facts of what he'd done, brother Myron caved. He admitted tricking Cletus into flipping the breaker switch in full knowledge the act would electrocute Travis' father. Unwilling to go down alone, he quickly pointed his finger at his uncle. Munch was the mastermind—right down to the method.

The final nail in the coffin came from an unexpected source. Eddie Hayes. He told the police that he heard what Munch said to Travis and Delaney that night in the bar. Word for word, he repeated his boss' confession to the police.

Tonya Hernandez was certain that Munch would be convicted. If he didn't plead guilty first to keep the death penalty at bay. Thirty years to life instead? Travis would never be happy. However, he felt justice had been served.

The sound of music made Travis stop in his tracks, a smile spreading across his face. As he walked past the kitchen toward the back of the house, he was taken back to the first time notes from a piano drew him—almost against his will—to a meeting that would change his life forever.

The door stood open. Travis leaned against the jamb and marveled at the woman he saw. Unlike that fateful evening eleven years earlier, she didn't try to hide her talent. Instead of slumped over the keys, her shoulders were pulled back, posture straight but relaxed. Her hair hung loosely around her shoulders, not wound into a tight knot.

And her eyes—those startlingly purple eyes—weren't hidden behind a pair of ugly, useless glasses. Bright. Clear. At the moment, a little dreamy as her fingers caressed the keys. From a myriad of choices, she somehow put the right sounds together to make a melody that touched something inside Travis the first time he heard her play.

He rubbed his chest—the spot just above his heart. Some things never change.

"Are you going to stand and stare at me all day?" Delaney asked without missing a beat.

"I can think of worse ways to spend my time."

Delaney slid to the side of the bench, making room. Travis joined her, his kiss lingering on her soft, fragrant cheek.

"One of yours," he asked.

"Something I'm fiddling with. I can't quite get the ending right."

"Sounded good to me."

Travis had always assumed Delaney would major in music. Psychology made sense—she'd found her calling. But he was glad she still played. And composed.

"I received an interesting email this morning."

"Good for you. Most of my emails are nothing but crap. Male enhancement cream? I don't think so."

Chuckling, Delaney ended the song with a small flourish.

"I can attest to the fact that you don't need any help in the enhancement department."

"Aw shucks. You'll make me blush." Travis fanned his face as if trying to cool the color as it rose in his cheeks. However, the twinkle in his eyes told a different story.

"You aren't the blushing type."

"Oh, I don't know."

"Please," Delaney scoffed. "Your face is too pretty, and your ego is too big."

Travis loved bantering with Delaney. Sharp as a tack with exactly his brand of humor, she easily—enthusiastically—matched him quip for quip. However, she had something else in mind. As he opened his mouth, she stopped his response, her lips covering his. Travis pulled her close. Kissing beat out banter any day of the week and twice on Sundays.

"Thank you," Delaney sighed, kissing him again.

"Tell me what I did so I remember to do it again. You give the best rewards."

"The email I mentioned? Seems *Alma's Heart* received a huge donation yesterday afternoon."

"Oh, that."

The shelter for abused women and children would carry the name of Delaney's mother. A tribute to the woman who ultimately saved her daughter but couldn't save herself. Travis wanted his gift to be anonymous. He should have known Delaney would find out.

"The check I sent to pay you back. You signed over the entire amount. And arranged to donate a sizable amount every year."

Travis shrugged. "Since you weren't supposed to pay me back, the money was never mine."

"And the yearly donation?"

"I believe in you." He touched Delaney's face. The look in her eyes made his heartbeat stutter. "And the cause you chose to champion. A little money thrown into the pot is the very least I can do."

"Hardly little."

"Depends on your point of view. Which reminds me." Travis' eyes narrowed. "I meant to ask, but with everything that happened,

I forgot. Where did you get the money to pay me back? Professionally, I know you've established a successful, growing practice. But you haven't had time to save *that* kind of cash."

Delaney shot him a look—one telling him she wished he hadn't asked.

"Some of the money I saved," she said. Standing, she moved to look out the window where Candice pitched a ball to her daughter. The sight of Emma, expression determined as she choked up on a bat almost as big as she was, made Delaney smile. Football was the traditional Thanksgiving sport. Not baseball.

Travis' influence had touched them all.

"Emma has quite a swing."

"You've been coaching her."

"I like to nurture young talent." Travis slid his arm around her waist. "About the check, Del? The money I sent was for you to spend."

"I did. At first." Delaney had been grateful. However, as soon as she could, she found a job. Added to her scholarship, within four years, she had' been able to support herself.

"I asked you to stop sending money—through your lawyer," she added, eyebrows raised. "He must have told you."

"He had a standing order. Send the checks once a week, without fail. No argument."

"If you'd called. Or written. Anything, I would've argued." Delaney could remember the times she'd longed to hear from Travis. And how she'd started to resent those damn weekly checks. "I thought about tearing them up. Until I realized somebody would've noticed the money was still in your account."

Delaney's solution had been simple. She saved the money so one day, she could return every dime.

"Like pulling teeth," Travis muttered. He led her across the room to a light-gray sofa. Sitting, he tugged her down beside him. "What about those first four years? I know the amount was sizable. Where did you get the money, Del?"

"Watch the tone there, buddy. I didn't stand on a street corner."

"Lovely, sexy Delaney," Travis smiled—all charm and twinkling eyes—as his lips caressed the palm of her hand. "If you ever decided to sell your body, you could charge the moon, and the price wouldn't be high enough."

"Ah. You are so sweet." Delaney sighed. "And so full of crap."

Travis chuckled. He'd never known a woman like her. "We can both shovel the shit when we want."

"Okay. You want the truth?" She took a deep breath. "I wrote a jingle."

"Say again?"

"A jingle. A catchy song, specifically written to sell a product."

"I know what a jingle is, smartass."

"How was I supposed to know," Delaney reasoned. "You seemed a bit confused by the concept."

"The concept is clear as glass. Your participation in the process threw me off a bit. Care to explain?"

"A friend clued me into a contest. Write a jingle. Make a few bucks." Delaney made the whole thing sound like an everyday occurrence. "What did I have to lose? In about an hour, I had the tune, a few silly words. I forgot the whole thing until I received a phone call. I'd won. End of story."

The woman could talk for hours—and he loved to listen. He couldn't figure out why she was suddenly so reticent.

"Throw me an epilogue. Would I know the jingle?"

"Maybe."

"Are you embarrassed? What's the product?" Travis searched his brain. "Tampons? Feminine twat deodorant?"

Delaney snorted—half laugh, half cough. "I can't believe you used the word twat. If you *ever* had the impulse to blush, now would be the time."

The expression on Delaney's face was priceless. Travis felt his lips twitch

"Wrong word? I'm open to a better choice. Pussy? Or—"

"*Puppy Bites*," Delaney shouted. "The jingle was for *Puppy Bites*."

Travis let out a low whistle. Whether they used the product or not, everybody knew the *Puppy Bites* jingle. Every time he turned on the television or radio, the commercial was on.

"How rich are you, Del?" Travis only half-teased. Advertising was big business. The endorsement deals he'd cut made him a small fortune. "Richer than me?"

"Hardly. I'm comfortable. So, rest easy. I want your body, not your money."

"Good to know." Travis pulled his shirt over his head.

"What are you doing?"

"Giving you what you want," he said as he unbuttoned his jeans.

Delaney took a moment as if weighing her options. Finally, she smiled.

"Okay, stud. But close the curtains unless you want Emma to get a gander at your male bits and pieces."

Travis did as Delaney asked, dropping his pants and underwear in one fluid motion. Her eyes turned a deep, appreciative amethyst. Grinning, he spread his arms.

"For your eyes only."

CHAPTER SEVENTEEN

● ≈ ● ≈ ●

FOR THE FIRST time in Delaney's life, she wished she wasn't quite so smart. A high I.Q. was great. Professionally, her keen intelligence had taken her a long way. And would take her even further. Most of the time, she was quite literally the smartest person in the room.

Delaney glanced at the manila envelope that lay on the bed, cursing herself. She'd thought herself into a corner, and for the life of her, she didn't know how to get out.

A big, working overtime brain was great—until it wasn't.

"I don't have to go through with my plan."

Delaney spoke to an empty room, but she always talked to herself when trying to reason out a problem. *Other* people's problems. She could stand back, observe, analyze. Psychiatry was a fluid science. However, when she found the right path, she never wavered from her course.

Why could she help others with such certainty, yet now that she was involved, she questioned what had seemed like the perfect solution?

Physician heal thyself? Sure. Right. No problem.

"Do you feel like going out for lunch?" Travis walked into her bedroom. "Since this is our last day, I thought we could grab a bite someplace and take a leisurely walk around town after."

A month had passed since Delaney had returned to Green Hills. Less than a week later, Travis showed up—ready to do battle. So much had happened. So much had changed. Last night, they lay in bed talking about the future. *Their* future.

Nothing had been written in stone. Washington State and Hawaii weren't exactly around the corner from each other. But they knew what they had was too important not to make things work.

Delaney cursed herself. And she cursed the United States Postal Service. If only that damn envelope had arrived twenty-four hours later. She could have pretended she hadn't set something in motion that could blow her relationship with Travis into a million unfixable pieces.

"What's this?" Travis asked, picking up the yellow envelope before flopping onto the bed.

"Nothing." A mistake. Or not. Why the hell couldn't she make up her mind? "Are you sure you want to leave your motorcycle behind?"

"Pete's happy to store the bike in his garage until the next time I'm here." Travis laughed. "Never thought I'd hear myself say those words. Or mean them."

"I know what you mean. Since neither of us is free for Christmas, Candice expects us next year."

Trace casually examined the outside of the envelope. Eyebrows rising when he spotted the return address.

"What did you say?"

"Maybe?" Delaney's fingers itched to grab the package from him. "A lot can happen in a year."

"True." Travis put the envelope flat on his palm as if testing the weight. "Is there something you want to tell me, Del? Something to do with why you've received a rather hefty piece of correspondence from your lawyer?"

Delaney could have stopped him. Travis gave her plenty of time to protest as he opened the flap. The bundle slid onto the bed, giving her one last chance to change her mind. But she remained silent, holding her breath as he picked up the papers and began to read.

Travis didn't get far—the first paragraph said everything he needed to know.

"What the hell is this?"

Meeting his puzzled gaze, Delaney took a deep breath. Maybe she was too smart for her own good. But she was determined to plow forward, hoping she was right.

"Travis. I want a divorce."

"SPRING TRAINING. GOD'S way of punishing all the bad boys who didn't exercise and eat right over the off season."

Travis grunted in response to Nick Sander's comment. His friend always complained during the early workouts before the games began. But this year, Nick seemed particularly prickly.

Another time, Travis would have joked a smile out of Nick. Not this time. He was mired in a black humor of his own and wasn't in the mood to play the clown.

As he sprinted up and down the field, Travis tried to concentrate on the task at hand—getting ready for a long, grueling baseball season. But his body was too conditioned to the routine to give his mind a rest. As his feet pounded the turf at the Cyclones' complex in Arizona, his thoughts were in Hawaii. With Delaney.

Travis, I want a divorce.

At first, Travis was certain he'd heard wrong. Or the whole thing was a joke. But the papers were right there in his hand—and Delaney wasn't laughing.

"Why?" he'd asked, unable to wrap his head around the concept.

After everything they'd been through? The years apart when one of them could have ended their marriage at any time but didn't? They'd faced the past, battled their demons, and come out the other side. Stronger. Together.

Or so Travis thought.

Now, when the future seemed brighter than ever, Delaney wanted a divorce? What the hell!

"If we don't start fresh, we'll never know if we stayed married for the right reasons," she explained. "What if a month from now, when you've had time to take a breath—time away from me. What if you realized you've made a terrible mistake?"

Travis had tried his best to follow Delaney's reasoning. She was the one with the fancy degree. But the longer he listened, the crazier she sounded.

"Of all the convoluted, asinine, wrong-headed ideas." He could either pace, or put his fist through the door. "When did you contact your lawyer?"

"The day before the election."

Three weeks? Travis stopped, tossed his hands in the air, then resumed pacing.

"And you didn't think to mention the fact to me? You decided, on your own. What I think—what I want—doesn't matter."

"You're wrong. I—"

"You don't have a very high opinion of me." Frustrated, Travis gave his scalp a hard rub. About time for another haircut. Guess Delaney wouldn't be around to do the job.

"Do you think I can't keep my dick in my pants?"

Delaney sighed, her eyes troubled. For a moment, Travis thought she'd come to her senses. He was wrong.

"I don't want you to have any regrets."

"You keep talking about me. What I need. What I want. How about you, Del? Maybe you're the one with the doubts."

"Maybe I am."

Delaney's answer had taken the wind out of Travis' outraged sails. He could argue about how he felt. How he was all in. Dedicated to her—to them. But if she wasn't on the same page? Nothing he could say would matter.

"Sign the papers, Travis. Spend the next few months thinking about us. I'll do the same. Once the divorce is final, we'll be free to decide if we want to be together."

Travis had to admit, Delaney was good at her job. So cool and calm. She almost made sense. *Almost*. He let her go without making another attempt to change her mind.

Then spent all of December and January stewing.

Part of him wanted to get on a plane, track Delaney down, and end the farce she'd started. Anger and a big dose of pride kept him in Seattle. Alone, for the most part—unless Spencer dragged him out for a drink.

Other women didn't interest him—if Delaney were there, he'd laugh in her face. *Take that*, he'd tell her. *I only want you.*

Turned out the joke was on him. Travis had done the worst thing possible. He'd fallen in love with his wife.

Travis pulled to a stop barely out of breath while most of his teammates were bent over, sucking oxygen. At least one positive had come out of the mess he placed firmly on Delaney's shoulders. He'd spent so much time at the gym to take out his frustrations—lifting weights, punching bags, swimming laps—he was in the best shape of his life.

"You want to tell me why you have a bug lodged up your ass?" Spencer, sweat dripping down his face, tossed Travis a bottle of water.

"Nope."

Travis kept walking, straight into the clubhouse. If he couldn't talk to Delaney, he wasn't talking. Period.

"What's his problem?" Nick asked, wiping his face.

Spencer wasn't blind. Travis *and* Nick were hurting. Both mired deep in woman troubles. A subject he knew something about. At one time—before he wised up—he'd been an expert.

Unfortunately, his best friends weren't interested in availing themselves of his vast knowledge. He'd keep trying. Because that's what buddies did.

"What's your problem?"

Spencer crossed his arms and waited. The look—raised eyebrow, steady gaze with just the right combination of steel and sympathy—was magic at getting people to open up. But now and then, even Spencer Kraig's patented magic failed.

"Fuck off, Kraig."

Nick followed Travis into the clubhouse. Spencer closed his eyes, head tipped back in defeat.

"It's going to be a long, fucking spring."

TRAVIS TOSSED HIS keys onto the kitchen counter. The house was small, dark, but serviceable—windows and natural light at a premium. A temporary place to crash. He'd considered himself lucky to find a rental on Lake Washington, close to the lot where his future home was currently under construction. Another plus? He was within walking distance of Spencer and Nick's houses.

Today, Travis didn't want company. Especially his own. He was bone tired—body and soul. As he walked toward the bedroom, leaving a trail of clothing in his wake, he hoped sleep would come. He was sick and tired of staring at the ceiling, the same loop of thoughts and recriminations circling his brain.

Another Spring Training was in the books. The regular season was set to begin the day after tomorrow. He was ready. Travis never let his private life interfere with his job. Once he stepped onto the field, his focus was laser sharp. Between the lines, baseball had always come first. Always would.

The problem was, Travis couldn't spend twenty-four hours a day at the ballpark. Right now, he had something else to think about. The little gift he'd received that morning before he left Arizona.

His divorce from Delaney was official.

Travis scrubbed a hand over his face. He'd signed the papers as she asked. But for some inexplicable reason, he'd expected her to change her mind. He should have known better.

For what had to be the hundredth time since landing in Seattle, Travis checked his phone. Pete called. Nothing important. Spencer—naturally. He scrolled through the messages. No Delaney.

Would she call? Or had she decided a life without him was a better fit?

Naked, Travis crawled into bed. He could live without Delaney. But better? No. Absolutely not. For him, she was the perfect fit.

SEVEN-THIRTY. TRAVIS blinked at the bedside clock, frowning. PM or AM? Didn't matter, he decided. If he'd slept five hours or fifteen, he wasn't ready to get up.

With a sigh, he started to close his eyes. But an arm sliding around him from behind had them popping open. All of a sudden, Travis was wide awake.

"I'll understand if you want to throw me out. Just let me have my say first."

Delaney. He knew before she said a word, but was afraid his imagination had played a nasty trick on him.

"Am I dreaming?" he asked. Better to be sure.

"No." A kiss brushed against his skin.

"Are you naked?"

"Yes." He felt her lips curve into a smile.

"How did you get in?"

"Spencer."

Yoda. He should have known.

"Okay." Travis took Delaney's hand, tugging at her arm until her soft, warm body molded to his back. "I've been waiting for a long time, Del. You better have something good to say."

Her scent—clean and sexy—washed over him. Before she said a word, Travis felt himself start to relax, as if he could breathe for the first time in over four months.

"I screwed up."

Travis smiled. "So far, so good."

"Have you ever found yourself talking, knowing everything you said was pure crap? Yet, try as you might, you couldn't stop the flow." Delaney kissed him again, her breath sweet against his neck as she rested her chin on the slope of his shoulder. "That day in Green Hills? I had a speech planned. Clinical. Logical. I felt outside my body. Floating above, screaming at myself to shut up."

"You didn't listen. To yourself, or to me."

"No. And I paid the price. I've been miserable, Travis."

"Join the club."

"Really?"

Delaney sounded so pleased, he had to chuckle.

"I'm glad my pain makes you happy."

"Never." Delaney squeezed closer. "I was afraid you hadn't missed me."

"Missed you? Nah. Only every second of every day."

"Can you forgive me?"

Travis turned. Maybe he was in the middle of a dream. He'd lost track of the times he'd imagined Delaney exactly as he found her. Naked. In his bed. Her head on his pillow. Leaning over, he turned the light on low. And those eyes. A brilliant purple shining just for him.

If he dreamed, he never wanted to wake.

"I have a few questions."

Better answered with Delaney in his arms. With a hum of happiness, she settled close.

"Shoot."

"If you knew you'd made a mistake, why did you let the divorce go through? Why not call me? Or come to see me? I would've welcomed you with open arms."

"I spent most of December and January wallowing."

"Good word." Travis could relate.

Delaney smiled. Her hand touched his arm. Then his chest. His face. As though she had to reassure herself he was there. "I was too stubborn to admit—to anybody, even myself—that I was so wrong a new word needs to be invented to describe my wrongness."

"Grab a thesaurus, genius girl. The words are already out there."

"I imagine you've called me a name or two I'd rather not hear."

Travis shrugged. Another time he might share a few of the colorful curse words he'd directed her way. But not here. Not now.

"What happened in February?"

"A friend gave me a firm talking to. She was tired of the way I moped around. And I quote. *'You threw away a man who wants to spend his life with you? A man who treats you right? Who isn't hard on the eyes and is great in bed? Are you out of your mind?'* My answer was yes. I was out of my mind."

"I want to meet your friend. She sounds like a very smart lady."

"She is."

"And then?" Travis asked. "What happened after your epiphany?"

"March was a busy month. I lost track of time—and the divorce. I received the final papers yesterday."

"Mine arrived this morning."

Delaney nodded, gaze steady.

"Even if I'd remembered in time, I wouldn't have stopped the divorce."

"Why not?" Travis wasn't in the mood for another of Delaney's theories.

"Because, if we were still married, I couldn't do this."

Rising to her knees, gloriously naked, Delaney took his hand in hers, holding them near her heart.

"You were my friend when I had none. Saved me when I needed saving."

"You did the same for me," Travis reminded her. Certain where Delaney was headed, he sat up so he could look into her bright purple eyes.

"You became my lover when the time was right. I hope you'll be by my side, no matter what, for the rest of my life. I love you. I always have. Travis Forsythe? Will you marry me?"

"Yes."

Laughing, Delaney fell into his embrace. As he reverently touched her face, his mouth brushed hers before deepening the kiss. Long. Slow. Heartfelt.

"I love you, Del."

"Forever?" she whispered.

"Forever."

Travis didn't believe in destiny. Or fate. Or chance. He believed in Delaney.

EPILOGUE

● ≈ ● ≈ ●

DELANEY COVERED HER eyes, unable to watch. Top of the ninth. The Cyclones were ahead by two. But the visiting team had the bases loaded with only one out. A base hit would almost guarantee a tie game. A double to the gap, the Cyclones would lose their lead.

She couldn't look. Well, maybe a peek.

"The outcome will be the same whether you watch or not. Put your hands down and enjoy the show."

Jordyn Kraig popped a peanut into her mouth. Though they only met that afternoon, Delaney and Spencer Kraig's sister had clicked immediately. Funny and a bit irreverent, Jordyn was also gorgeous. A trait all Travis' friends seemed to share.

Seats to opening day were impossible to come by. Jordyn had originally planned to watch at home. But as a favor to Travis, she agreed to squire Delaney through her first professional baseball game.

Jordyn—despite her blasé attitude—was a blast to be around. She knew the game in and out. And didn't mind answering Delaney's endless questions.

Delaney lowered her hands as Jordyn suggested, gripping her program for dear life.

"How can you be so calm?"

"One hundred and sixty-two games, that's how. Not counting the post-season. Knock wood. You have to pace yourself." Jordyn grinned when the crowd booed the next batter. "I will admit. There's something special about opening day. I'm glad I came."

Delaney nodded, her eyes on the field—and Travis. His once pristine white uniform was streaked with dirt—a testament to how hard he played. He ran the bases hard—full speed all the way. His defense was exemplary. And his bat? Three hits and two RBIs told the tale.

She'd always loved watching him on television. But nothing compared to the thrill of Travis, live and in person.

Knowing she'd end the evening in his arms added an extra layer of excitement.

"Dubois is a threat to hit one out every time he steps to the plate." Completely lost in the moment, Jordyn forgot about popping peanuts.

A home run was bad enough. But a grand slam? Delaney didn't know if her heart could take much more.

"Keep the ball low and away," Jordyn muttered. "Low and away."

Delaney couldn't tell one pitch from another. All she wanted was to see the final out. Now!

As the ball left the pitcher's hand, Delaney watched as Travis shifted to his left. She heard the crack of the bat and before she could blink, Travis dove, body outstretched as far as possible. He hit the ground just as the ball hit his glove. Rolling to his knee, he flipped the ball to Nick Sanders for the force at second.

Game over. With a scream of joy, Delaney jumped in the air.

Travis, grinning, celebrated the victory with his teammates. Her man. Her warrior.

"Well," Jordyn shouted. "What did you think?"

Delaney hugged her new friend.

"Best time ever."

A hundred and sixty-one more games? Every season? A life by Travis' side—no matter what? Delaney could hardly wait.

COMING IN OCTOBER

● ● ●

**FOR THE FIRST TIME**

ONE STRIKE AWAY BOOK FOUR

TURN THE PAGE FOR A SNEAK PEEK AT
THE EXCITING SPORTS ROMANCE SERIES
ONE PASS AWAY

AFTER THE RAIN
(One Pass Away Book One)

PROLOGUE

LOGAN. LOGAN. LOGAN.

Logan Price closed his eyes, taking it all in.

"Hear that, kid?" Starting quarterback Gaige Benson slapped him on the back. "Two games under your belt and you're a star. Now let's go out there and add super to the front of it."

The announcer for the team set them in motion down the tunnel with his familiar introduction.

"And now, let's hear it for your division champion SEATTLE KNIGHTS."

The roar of the crowd. There was nothing like it. A packed stadium. Fans chanting his name. Few people would ever experience what it was like to take the field in a professional football game.

Logan Price had been working for this his entire life. He could still remember in exact detail the first game he ever saw. Too small to climb onto the stool in his father's bar by himself, his old man had lifted him onto the seat.

Stay and be quiet.

Not an easy order to follow for an active, inquisitive little boy. One look at the game and for once, Logan had no problem following his father's command. The old TV transported him to a foreign world filled with bright lights and shiny helmeted warriors. Logan didn't know what he was watching. He did know he wanted to be one of those men.

A Sunday afternoon in rural Oklahoma. Lefty's Pub was filled with after-church drinkers who figured they had done their duty to God and family. The rest of the day was their time. A beer. Or two. Or six. Cronies who understood a man's need to unwind before the start of another workweek.

And football.

If the Friday night high school game was their true religion, the Sunday afternoon games were a close second. As Oklahoma boys, they hated anything Texas. The men of Denville gathered every week to root for whichever team was playing the Dallas Cowboys.

No matter how the games ended. Whether the crowd was happy or disgruntled. It meant more drinking. Hours later, husbands, boyfriends, and sons would stumble out, pile into beat-up trucks, and weave their way home to frustrated wives, girlfriends, and mothers.

As he grew older, Logan's view changed. He moved from the stool to behind the bar. And he promised himself one thing. He would never become one of those men. He wouldn't spend the week at a job he hated. His home wouldn't be a semi-wide trailer filled with hand-me-down furniture and a wife to whom he couldn't face going home.

His Sundays were going to be spent playing football, not watching it.

"Ready to take down this vaunted Arizona defense?" Gaige yelled at him, butting helmets.

Vaunted. Good word, Logan thought. His QB liked to use what his granny called highfalutin talk. Must have been that Ivy League education. He knew that Gaige Benson didn't grow up with a silver spoon in his mouth. He came from the mean streets of Brooklyn. He had the scars to prove it.

Like Logan, Gaige had vowed to get out of the life into which he was born. In the process, he polished himself up like a new penny. He took advantage of his full-ride scholarship to Yale. He didn't spend all his time on the football field. Fancy vocabulary. Fancy clothes. Fancy women. They were all part of the package Gaige purposefully fashioned for himself.

Seventeen years after clawing his way out of the tenement that he grew up in, very little of that borough-rat remained. Until game time. No one was tougher than Gaige Benson. Three-time league MVP. Considered one of the best ever to play the game. No one stood in his way when he was playing the game. He had the scars to prove it.

"Gather round."

Knights head coach Harry Coleman gathered the team close. He had to yell over the crowd, but he had the voice to do it. Booming was putting it mildly. The first time Logan heard it, he stood right beside the man. The ringing in his ears didn't go away for three days.

"Divisional game. If I have to say any more than that, you shouldn't be out here. Go kick some ass."

The defense took the field to start the game. Arizona had a rookie quarterback drafted in the second round from a small college in the Midwest. The only reason he was out there was because the regular starter suffered a concussion in last week's game and the regular backup had food poisoning. Thrown into action at the last minute, Logan swore he could see the guy's hands shaking before he took the first snap. When the ball went sailing between his legs, Logan shook his head.

The moment was too big for some people. For Logan, it wasn't big enough. He aimed for the biggest stage of all. The Super Bowl. It wasn't a matter of if he would get there, but when.

"Three and out." Gaige grinned, pulling on his helmet. "Come on, kid. Let's go show them how it's done."

Logan ran onto the field. Kid. He shook his head, grinning. From the first day of training camp, Gaige had hung that moniker on him. Ironic since he was almost twenty-five, a good two years older than most of the other rookies. However, he supposed when someone had been in the league as long as Gaige, all the new guys seemed like kids.

"We're starting on the ground," Gaige instructed them in the huddle. "Sweep out left. Basic. Got it?"

Lining up as he had a thousand other times, Logan checked the defense. He knew he was fast. One of the fastest in the game. What set him apart was his anticipation. He had the uncanny ability to read the guy covering him. He knew when to fake left or when to fake right. Stutter step or flat out, in your face, catch me if you can.

His speed got him out of Denville, Oklahoma. His brains and determination got him to the NFL.

The sounds of the game were as familiar to Logan as the back of his own hand. The call from scrimmage. Each quarterback had his own unique cadence. Gaige was a master of mixing his up. Study him all you want. Good luck figuring it out. His teammates knew. A signal just before they broke the huddle.

Pay attention, you were golden. Slack off even once? Gaige could ream a guy out with the best of them. And he had no problem doing it in the middle of the game.

An entire YouTube channel had been devoted to Gaige and his rants. They were as legendary as the man himself. With a ball in his hand, he was cool as ice. The rest of the time, watch out.

No one would ever accuse Logan of lacking focus. Today was no exception. They were driving down the field. First and ten from the Arizona twenty-yard line. He already had three carries of thirty-five yards. It was going to be a good day.

"Ready to take it in?" Gaige asked.

"Always."

"Then show them what you've got."

A quick snap later, Gaige handed the ball to Logan. The offensive line created a seam. Not a big one. Just big enough. Using the push of his powerful legs, Logan surged through. One more step. They wouldn't catch him. No one could.

Like everything connected with the game, Logan heard the snap of the bone with total clarity. The agony that surged through his body was so intense he almost passed out. In the next few minutes, he was going to wish he had.

"Get back." Logan heard Gaige through the haze of pain. "Goddamn it. Move the hell off."

The three-hundred-and-fifty-pound linebacker didn't get off by standing. He rolled. Crushing Logan's broken leg as he went. He would never know if the move had been deliberate. Now, it was the last thing on his mind. He only cared about two things. How bad was the injury and when would he be able to play again.

"Hold on, kid." Gaige took his hand. "They're bringing the stretcher."

The team doctor checked his eyes. Logan knew he was asked some questions. What they were and how he answered, he would never remember. By the time they carted him off the field, Logan knew the break was bad.

"Gaige." Logan reached for him.

"I'm here, kid."

"Is it over?"

"The game?" Gaige walked with him, his head bent toward Logan. "No. But I promise we're going to win the bastard."

They loaded him onto the open cart. They had him secured and the vehicle rolled away before Logan had his answer. He wasn't wondering about the game. It was his career.

To no one in particular, he whispered the question again.

"Is it over?"

CHAPTER ONE

LOGAN SAT UP in bed, his body covered with a fine coating of sweat.

He glanced at the clock. Three in the fucking morning. On the one night he managed to get to bed at a reasonable hour, he was plagued by the nightmare that had haunted his dreams for the past two years.

Running his hand through his long, damp hair, Logan fell back onto the mattress. His sheets were as wet as he was. With a grimace, he rolled onto the floor. Flexing his stiff knee, he stripped the bed, tossing everything onto a pile of dirty clothes he planned on taking to the laundromat on his day off.

There was an alternative. He could always take Linda Sue Hemmings up on her offer. She would do his laundry anytime. Payment. On-call stud service whenever her husband Darryl was out of town on business. As much as Logan hated folding socks, he decided the price was too high. He had lost a lot in the last few years. He still held onto his dignity. Just barely.

Still groggy, Logan shuffled to the bathroom. Flipping on the light, he grimaced at what the mirror reflected.

Too many late nights followed by not enough sleep. As patterns went, it wasn't a healthy one. Perpetually bloodshot eyes.

Dark circles on his dark circles. He needed a haircut. Logan ran his hand over his face. Even more, he needed a shave.

He had to hand it to himself. When he let himself go, he went all the way. All he had to do was stop showering. If he wasn't worried about driving the customers away with his smell, he might have considered it.

The old plumbing rattled with protest when he turned on the faucet. It wasn't a bad place. There were worse. Logan splashed some cold water on his face. He didn't bother with a towel. It would dry soon enough on its own.

He had two choices.

Toss and turn for a couple of hours on the unmade bed – he really needed to get more than one set of sheets.

Or lose himself with an old friend.

Sleep wasn't coming which made the choice an easy one.

Logan pulled on a pair of old shorts, a faded t-shirt and sweatshirt that was too ratty to be called anything as fashionable as a hoodie. After lacing up his sneakers, he hit the road. When he was a kid, he ran for the fun of it. In high school and college, it strengthened his legs and improved his stamina. Now, the only thing it accomplished was getting him a reputation as that half-crazy Price boy. Running the deserted streets at all hours? Maybe his head had been permanently injured along with his leg.

Logan jogged past *Lefty's Pub*. The place where he spent most evenings tending bar. The day he left for college he swore to anyone who would listen that he had served his last beer. Eight years later, here he was, washing glasses and putting up with not so subtle jabs about how the mighty had fallen.

Coming back to Denville was more of an adjustment than Logan anticipated. He expected the cracks about his failed NFL career. Any kind of success tended to breed a certain amount of jealousy and resentment. There were those who reveled in his injury.

Logan Price always thought too much of himself. Denville wasn't good enough for the high school's star running back. He forgot all about us when he made it big.

The sound of his feet pounding on the unpaved side street couldn't keep the usual thoughts from creeping back. Some of what those people said was true. He had been full of himself. At seventeen, one wasn't written up in national magazines without it going to his head.

Logan never tried to hide his plans. A full-ride scholarship to the college of his choice. Then the pros. MVP awards. Super Bowl rings. The cocky attitude of a teenager wasn't any easier to take than if he had been an adult. Most of Denville embraced their golden boy.

AFTER ALL THESE YEARS
(One Pass Away Book Two)

PROLOGUE

SEAN McBRIDE WOKE up with a smile on his face. It happened a lot lately. And he thoroughly approved.

He stretched his long, athletic body. Some mornings every inch of him ached. Such was the life of a professional football player. Everything was about preparing for the game. Focus. Concentration. The goal was to be ready for game day.

He had to hold it together for sixty minutes. Pull out a win any way possible. Sacrifice his body to the football Gods and pray he walked away healthy enough to do it all again next week.

Sean dreaded the day after the game. The adrenaline had long ago worn off and he felt all of his thirty years. There were degrees of bad. Sometimes he shuffled to the shower, the aches and pains palpable, but mercifully bearable.

Then there were the bad days. After a day of three-hundred-pound defensive backs using him as their own personal punching bag, he didn't get out of bed—he crawled.

Bruised from top to bottom, his joints creaked and his muscles protested like screeching banshees. Those were the times he wondered why he did it. He could have been a doctor. Or a lawyer. He could have taken his father's advice and gone into the family business. No seventeen-year-old with dreams of glory in the NFL wanted to think about becoming a butcher. But damn. Cutting meat sounded good on those mornings.

This was a good Monday. His body felt lithe—limber. The bruises were there. That was part of his life. However, yesterday had been one of those rare games when every moment fell into place. From the kickoff to the final whistle, the outcome of the game was never in question.

Sean caught every ball thrown his way. He evaded the defense. Fast as the wind. Three touchdowns. One hundred and eighty-two total yards. A damn good day for any wide receiver. He would have had more if Coach Coleman hadn't taken him out of the game in the fourth quarter. With a big lead, there was no reason to risk injury when he wasn't needed.

The after-game celebration moved from the locker room to one of the team's favorite hangouts. Naturally the atmosphere was raucous. Cautiously so.

The Knights were having a stellar season. Ten wins, two losses. Sean and his friends had enough games under their belts to understand how quickly that could turn. Injuries tended to come in bunches. So far, they were healthy. However, that was bound to change. The hope was to get to the playoffs with all their major players on the roster.

After the game, they had a few drinks. Three was Sean's limit these days. A few years ago it was a different story. He would have closed the place down after a win. He and his bed partner of the moment would have moved on to someone's apartment, partying until dawn before going back to her place and fucking like demented rabbits. Then he would go home alone and catch a few hours sleep until it was time to grab a quick shower before heading to the Knights' headquarters to review film from the game.

Those days were over. Sean wasn't a kid anymore, high on his own press clippings and more testosterone than brains. Not that he had settled down completely. He could still party with the best of them. However, he chose his moments—ones that never took place during the season.

Women were another matter. Sean liked sex. Always had. If there were a God, he always would. While his bed partners weren't as varied, they were almost as frequent.

Sean knew players who abstained a few days before the game, saving their *juice*. He wasn't one of them. Sean had plenty of juice, thank you very much. Sex was necessary for a happy and healthy mind. For *his* happy and healthy mind.

A big plus to having sex at night was sex the next morning. It was one of his favorite things. A partner, warm and willing.

The perfect way to start the day.

Speaking of which. Smiling, Sean turned over. His hand reached out, expecting to find a soft, sweet woman. Instead, he found cold sheets. Sitting up, he looked around the room. Like the bed, empty. The bathroom door was open and the light off.

Not bothering to cover up, Sean jumped out of bed. Buck naked, he searched the house. She wasn't in the kitchen. Why would she be? She didn't cook, not even coffee. She was on a first-name basis with half the baristas in Seattle.

Was that it? Would she be back soon with two cups of steaming black caffeine and his favorite muffins? Sean was talking himself into that scenario when he saw the note.

He picked up the paper that had been propped against the lamp by the front door.

Sean.

Thank you for the past few weeks. After years of building it up in my mind, I was worried that it couldn't live up to my expectations. I should have known better. It was everything I had hoped for—and more.

We didn't make any promises. No strings were attached that need to be broken. After all these years, you can finally breathe easy. It's over. We are now friends without the expectation of benefits.

When we see each other, it will be as if it, we, never happened.

Sean read the note. Then read it again.

What the fuck? What was in those drinks?

Sean searched his memory for some kind of clue. The bar. His teammates. Then she was there. They laughed. Everything was smooth and easy. They seemed to be developing a rhythm. In his mind, they were together. Not a man and a woman—a couple.

It sounded good to him. He would have sworn she felt the same. He didn't want another woman. He wanted her. In his arms. In his life.

No expectations? Hell. He woke up with plenty of them, only to find out he was alone. Alone in bed. Alone. Period.

Sean scrubbed a hand over his face. He remembered the way she tasted. The way she melted into his arms. The curves of her luscious body pressed against his. Her sighs. His belief he would never get enough of her.

Crumpling the note into a ball, Sean tossed it across the room. Suddenly he felt every ache. His legs felt like lead. Slowly, he shuffled toward the bathroom. He needed a shower. Long and hot. Determined not to look at the bed, Sean's peripheral vision wouldn't let him off the hook that easily. It captured everything. The rumpled sheet. The pillow still holding the imprint of her head. A slash of red on the floor.

Frowning, Sean picked up the scrap of silk. So small he wondered why she had bothered. The image of her standing in nothing but her heels and the panties popped into his head. Unconsciously, his body tightened with desire.

Right, that was why.

Sean ran the smooth material over his cheek, feeling it catch on his morning stubble. He breathed deeply. He smelled vanilla and spice. Her essence. He would never forget it. As long as he lived, he would be able to close his eyes and conjure up her scent. Her taste.

His eyes popped open. *Friends? Nothing more? Bullshit*!

Keeping the panties in his hand, Sean headed for the shower. This wasn't over. Not by a long shot. It was just the beginning.

AFTER THE FIRE
(One Pass Away Book Three)

PROLOGUE

SHE HAD ONCE asked him if he believed in a higher power.

God? Buddha? Fairies dancing around a blazing fire late at night? Something. Anything bigger than us.

Gaige Benson hadn't known what to say. Not then. But as he stood in the empty open-air stadium—the stars lighting the evening sky—he knew the answer.

Football was his religion. The field he played on and the building surrounding it, his cathedral. If a higher power had a hand in it, then his answer was yes.

He believed.

Walking to the center of the field, Gaige took it all in. He found football at the age of thirteen. A boy who saw his future mapped out. Working in a factory. Drinking away his salary. Divorce. Doling out child support without maintaining a relationship with his children. A weekend father, who half the time didn't bother to show up.

The first time Gaige picked up a football, he felt a connection. The first time he threw it, it wobbled with the grace of a drunk leaving his favorite watering hole on a Saturday night. But it didn't matter. He threw the ball again. And again. Until he taught himself to make it spin in a perfect spiral.

At the time, Gaige didn't know his talent could be useful. Where he came from, Brooklyn kids didn't dream of bigger or better. Most of them didn't dream at all. Gaige was no different.

One day he was passing a playground when a football landed at his feet. The boys on the field yelled for him to toss it back. Without thinking, Gaige sent it sailing, a perfect strike. Then kept walking. He was wary of the man who ran after him. Strangers were the enemy—according to his father. They either wanted money or accused you of something you hadn't done.

Gaige took everything his father said with a big grain of salt. Don Benson didn't have a dime to his name. Why would anyone expect to get money from him? And if a man accused his father of something, chances were he was guilty.

But Gaige was a cautious boy. He fought when necessary and ran when he had no choice. The man trying to get his attention was big. His dark complexion didn't worry Gaige. In his experience, a man was either good or bad. The color of his skin had nothing to do with it.

It turned out that this man wasn't simply good. He was the best thing that ever happened to Gaige.

Terrance Aldridge coached the local Pop Warner football team. A boy with an arm like Gaige's shouldn't let his talent go to waste. Gaige listened. Play football? On a field? With other boys? Was such a thing possible? He didn't know if it were a scam—nor did he care. If there were the slightest chance, he would take it.

The only obstacle was getting a parent's permission. Terrance gave him the papers to be signed, telling Gaige to have his folks call him if they had any questions. Gaige didn't laugh aloud, but he wanted to. His mother never asked questions. Unless they were directed at his father. Wynona Benson hadn't made a move in fifteen years unless she received permission first.

His father was another matter. His word was law. Don Benson could do no wrong. If he drank too much and staggered home two days late, it was his right. If he backhanded his wife—just because—whose business was it? He earned the money. He made the rules. End of discussion.

Gaige hadn't asked his father because he knew what the answer would be. No! Not because he thought there was anything wrong with football. He watched it every Sunday—after laying down a bet that he never won. No, he wouldn't let Gaige play because he was a mean bastard who wanted everyone to be as miserable as he was.

Gaige got around it easily enough. He forged his father's signature. It wasn't the first time and it wouldn't be the last. There was no reason to think anyone would find out. His parents didn't care how he spent his days as long as the police didn't come knocking on the door.

He could steal. Lie. Cheat. Hell, his father wouldn't bat an eye at murder. *Do what you want as long as you don't get caught.* The mantra at the Benson house.

Gaige had no intention of his father finding out. He tried out for the team and made it. The money for equipment was another matter. Gaige didn't steal. Or cheat. Lying was a necessary evil. He would have done almost anything to play but it looked like his first and only dream would die before it had a chance.

Luckily, Terrance was able to dip into a discretionary fund to help boys like Gaige. It rankled to take charity. Especially when the other boys on the team had families to pay their way.

"Don't let it stop you, Gaige," Terrance told him. "Remember. And one day, when you have the means, pay it forward, son."

Twenty-five years later, Gaige hadn't forgotten that kindness and generosity. When he saw someone in need, he did something about it. Over the years, the *Gaige Benson Foundation* paid out millions of dollars to charities and individuals. He had filled the board with people he trusted and could count on to distribute the funds judiciously and without prejudice. The first man he had recruited was the man to whom Gaige owed everything—Terrance Aldridge. Friend. Father figure. Teacher.

"Hey, Gaige." Logan Price called out from high in the stands. "You coming? The guys are waiting to go to dinner."

"Five minutes."

Closing his eyes, Gaige breathed in the air. February in Texas. Tomorrow he would play in his first—and last Super Bowl. Win or lose, he was hanging up his cleats. He was thirty-eight years old. He had more money than he would ever need. He had won every award from Rookie of the Year to league MVP—four times.

This season he put everything on the line to get here— including the possibility that he had lost the only woman he had ever loved.

Gaige Benson was known for his razor-sharp focus. Any distractions off the field were left there as soon as the first whistle blew. It wouldn't be any different tomorrow. Nothing would get in the way.

His gaze drifted to the section where she would be sitting. If she showed up. Gaige planned on going out a winner. But what about the day after? Or the day after that? His future stretched out in front of him. He had plans in place. There were hundreds of options for him to consider.

Do you believe in a higher power?

Her voice and that question had haunted Gaige for almost sixteen years. If there were a God, he prayed the woman he loved

www.ingramcontent.com/pod-product-compliance
Lightning Source LLC
Chambersburg PA
CBHW071258170626
46809CB00001B/262

would find it in her heart to forgive him. He had a lot of years left. He didn't want to spend them alone.

In his lifetime, Gaige Benson had dreamt of only two things. Playing football. And loving Violet Reed.